I was caught up in a momentum; I knew sex was the next stage. That was the connection I wanted with him now. Every time we were together, I was bowled over by the way my body seemed to take over, to want more and more from him. I was tired of dreaming, fantasising – I wanted real experience. I'd had enough worrying and agonising. Supposing it does go wrong, I said to myself, supposing I sleep with him and then a few months later we split up – it won't be the end of the world. I'll have had that experience. I'll *know*.

We were both tense, waiting. It felt like we were waiting for ever. Nothing else was really important, beside it. And then we had this opportunity just landed on us . . .

from The Women's Press

Kate Cann lives in Twickenham with her husband, daughter, son and dog. She worked as a book editor for many years before writing *Diving In* (The Women's Press, 1996) and *In the Deep End*. She has also written a novel for the young adult list at Red Fox, and a book in the Life Education series for Watts publishers.

In the Deep
End

Kate Cann

First published by Livewire Books, The Women's Press Ltd, 1997
A member of the Namara Group
34 Great Sutton Street, London EC1V 0DX

British Library Cataloguing-in-Publication Data
A catalogue record for this book is available from the British Library

ISBN 0 7043 4948 5

Typeset in Bembo 12/14pt by MC Typeset Ltd, Kent
Printed and bound in Great Britain by Caledonian International

To Jeff

Preface

Art and I had a brief relationship. Seven weeks. I was completely obsessed with him, but I wasn't sure what he felt about me because communication wasn't his strong point. It wasn't just the way he looked I was mad on, although that was pretty blinding – it was the energy I felt from him. Sometimes it was so strong it was like being picked up and shaken. It didn't always feel good, the energy, but it had this addictive quality. I stopped wanting to be with anyone else but him.

I know now that he felt that energy just as strongly as I did, and I suppose it partly excuses what he did. Partly.

We went through wordless negotiations in those seven weeks. He wanted to have sex right away. I didn't. Just kissing him was unnerving enough. And meanwhile, I tried to get him to talk to me, to open up a bit. Gradually, I thought, we were drawing closer.

And then he asked me away for a family weekend, to this cottage his dad owns in the country. I was so happy about it. Until bedtime came round and I found everyone – including him – assumed I'd sleep in his room. Like his ranks and ranks of other girlfriends had done.

There's nothing seductive about being set up like that, especially when you've never slept with anyone before. I'd ended up screaming abuse at Art and sleeping downstairs on a couch. Then, when I'd got home, all destroyed and upset, my large, ferocious mum had gone round to his house and screamed abuse at the whole lot of them for their lack of moral fibre.

As far as ending relationships go, it was a pretty definite finish.

Probably the worst week of my life followed. I felt humiliated; I felt betrayed; and I missed him so much I could barely move. Then, that Saturday, I was slumped in McDonald's and Art walked in and sat opposite me. And, at last, he opened up to me. He said he was sorry about what had happened; he told me how much I meant to him, and asked me to give him another chance.

Well, what would you have done?

One

I'd arranged to meet Art that same evening, at a pub by the river. I was surprised by how calm I felt as I walked along there — sort of washed up, as though I'd survived a great disaster. Everything had cracked open between us, and this time I was determined it was going to stay open. This time we were going to talk.

Art was already there when I arrived, sprawled on a bench outside, staring into the river. The sight of him was so good I had to stop for a minute. Then I pushed my hands into my pockets and made myself walk on.

He looked up and saw me, and stood up, a bit awkwardly. 'Hi, Coll. Thanks for coming,' he muttered. 'I got you a drink.'

We sat down and I snatched up the glass and took a gulp. Inside, I was trembling. It was amazing to be sitting next to him again, feeling that energy again. 'That was

3

some coincidence, today,' I gabbled. 'Being at McDonald's at the same time. I mean, what are the statistical chances of two people –'

He shrugged. 'I knew you'd be there.'

'What d'you mean, you knew I'd be there?'

'I phoned your house – I spoke to your mum.'

So it hadn't been chance, I thought. He came after me.

'You spoke to – ? Shit. After the way she'd yelled at you and everything? You hero.'

'I tell you, Coll, I've never felt so scared in my life. I'd been trying to get the guts up to call all week. Then I nearly put the phone down when *she* answered. She sounded really mad. She said who the hell d'you think you are, ringing up, haven't you done enough damage ... and then I – I said I was sorry – and I just about begged her – I said I *had* to see you.'

I let out a sigh, wobbly with pleasure. 'And then ...?'

'She said you were out. Then she said I'd find you in McDonald's, and slammed the phone down.'

'Mum *told* you where I was? I can't believe it. She *loathes* you.'

'Thanks.'

'Well – maybe not loathes. But telling you where I was?'

'Maybe she thought it was our business. Maybe she thought you could handle it.'

'Maybe,' I said doubtfully. Mum wasn't good at leaving me to handle things. 'I s'pose if you'd said sorry and everything, she'd have weakened. I think it's your dad she blames most –'

'Good. Because last weekend was his fault.'

'*Sure* it was.'

'Honestly, Coll, your mum was right the way she laid into him. He's a real sleaze. It's no wonder I'm such a shit with a father like that.'

'Oh, *right*. So you inherited it, did you?'

'Yes. *And* I was brought up wrong. Other fathers go on about exam results – he wants to know how many girls I've pulled. He keeps a chart up in the kitchen.'

'Oh, be serious,' I said, laughing.

'I *am*. Sort of.'

I looked at the ground. 'Look, Art, it wasn't your dad who – lied to me,' I said.

'Oh, Coll, I didn't lie to you. I just didn't tell you –'

'The truth.'

' – what the set up was. Look, I know I behaved like a real jerk. But it wasn't just to get you to sleep with me.'

'Hah!'

'OK, it was. But it wasn't just sex. I mean you were – I was – I was going crazy. And it was so strong between us, and I thought – I wanted to get close to you.'

'You wanted to get close to me. Why didn't you *talk* about it, then? Find out what *I* felt?'

'Look, we've been through this. You were right, I was *embarrassed*, OK? I didn't know what the hell to say.'

I turned and stared at him. I still couldn't get my mind around the fact that, for him, taking all your clothes off and making love to someone for the first time was less embarrassing than just talking.

'I mean – sex is *mutual*,' I went on. 'Or it should be anyway. Not something you spring on someone without even – '

'Coll, I'm sorry I tried to push you into it,' he said, urgently. 'I got it all wrong and I'm sorry.'

5

'You made me feel like just someone to get laid – '

'Oh, God. It wasn't like that. I think you're *great*. I'm really – I'm completely gone on you. OK?'

'You didn't act it, Art,' I said faintly, as what he'd just said sunk into me. 'I mean I really did have no idea.'

'What d'you mean, act it? Buy you flowers and all that crap?'

'No – *no*! It's just – you seemed so distant some of the time. Quite a lot of the time. Nearly all of the time, actually. You seemed so shut off.'

'Well, if I was such lousy company, how come you kept seeing me?'

I laughed and turned to look at him, taking in every detail of his face – the line of his eyebrows, the line of his jaw, his mouth – and it was so obvious, I had to say it. 'Because you're a – because you're *gorgeous*.'

He grinned and moved closer to me. 'So are *you*, Coll. Completely gorgeous. You make me – Jesus, you make me – ' He broke off. I'd gone red with pleasure. 'Anyway,' he went on, 'I thought *you* were shut off. I mean – I love the way you talk and all the weird things you come out with, but sometimes it was like talking was all you wanted to do.'

There was a long pause. 'I suppose we were both coming in from – from different angles,' I said finally. I couldn't think of anything else to say.

'Give it another chance, Coll. Now this has happened we can – we can meet in the middle.'

I couldn't speak. He'd moved closer to me still, and I could smell the warm, cotton smell of his shirt, and I wanted more than anything to grab hold of him – to hold him.

Slowly, his hand moved across me and covered my hand. I stared at it. His long, strong fingers. His face was right next to mine now and I wanted to kiss him so badly my throat felt like it was closing up.

'Art, *why* couldn't you have said any of this before?' I squeaked.

'I don't know. Because I'm a loser.'

'You wouldn't talk before. You were all locked up.'

'Well, I'm talking now.'

There was a pause. Then there was a kind of mutual spring, and we were kissing.

Two

After several stupendous minutes, we resurfaced, and looked at each other.

'I'll – I'll go and get some more drinks,' Art croaked, and went into the pub. I sat and stared at the river eddying along, and I suddenly felt full of this wonderful, exhilarating confidence, and I realised I was giving myself full permission to get tied up with him again. Trust it, I said to myself. Well, *risk* it at any rate. That energy between you isn't fake.

Art came out and sat beside me, handing me my drink. 'So,' he said, 'was that like – a yes?'

'Might have been.'

'I know I was a real shit to you.'

'Yeah, you were,' I agreed, happily. 'I hated you.'

'I don't blame you. But now – '

'God, I *really* hated you. What a bastard, with your "It's

no big *deal*, Coll. You either want to or you don't."'

'Look, I admit it – I was a complete ...'

'And "We can fall asleep together afterwards." You weren't only a shit, you were corny, too. And making me sleep downstairs when I wouldn't sleep with you ...'

'Hang *on*, you ...'

'... and then being such a pig the next day. Refusing to say one word to me. I was so hurt. You really were a complete and utter bastard. You deserved to *die*.'

I sat back, smiling. I'd enjoyed that. Art was staring at me, eyes narrowed, starting to smile. It was funny, repeating what had nearly killed me at the time. It hardly hurt at all now.

'I was upset, too,' he said, leaning towards me. 'I felt rejected.'

'*Rejected?!!*'

'No bloke likes to be pushed away like that. It makes him insecure ... about his sexuality.'

'HA!! You – Mr Superstud? Nothing short of castration would start to make *you* feel insecure about your ...'

'You were savage. Screaming at me like that. Saying I was bullying you.'

'Well, you were.'

'Look, I've changed,' he said, suddenly serious again. 'I really have. I won't pressure you any more. We'll take it slow. I promise I – I won't jump on you any more.'

I started to laugh. That promise struck me as incredibly funny. 'Art,' I said, 'you don't imagine I'd go out with you for your *brain*, do you?'

He looked taken aback for a second – then he grinned. And I got hold of his hand, leaned over and kissed him again.

*

9

At the end of the evening Art walked back with me and we kissed a lot more outside my house. And it was so much better than even the best from before.

'Oh, God,' he said into my neck. 'I thought I'd blown it with you. I really thought I had. It feels so *good* just to touch you again ... just to ...'

'You back off,' I said, pulling away. 'You're lucky I'm even kissing you.'

'OK,' he said, humbly. 'I know I'm lucky.' Then he tried to get hold of me again.

I laughed, and pulled away, and said I had to go in.

I went upstairs and ran a very large, hot bath. Then I lay in the water and let it cover me, face and everything, and blew a series of bubbles into the water.

I felt so good it was almost unbearable. I stretched out every muscle in my body, admiring my legs, and my feet, and then I relaxed again.

- Point 1, I said to myself. Art's gone on you, he said so. He phoned your house; he came after you.
- Point 2. But one week ago he set you up in the worst kind of manipulative, lying-sod way. He was *unforgivable*!
- Point 3. You seem to have forgiven him. Already.
- Point 4. He is gorgeous. He is fit, he is lean, he has a face designed by an angel. I can't think straight when I'm near him. It's going to be all right. My instinct says.
- Point 5. Never mind your instinct — what about your brain? Think about it. No one changes that completely. And he goes through girls like a — well, he goes through loads of girls.

- Point 6. I don't care. I'm hooked on him. I just want to see him again.
- Point 7. But you have to set what you want against what's *sensible*.
- Point 8. No contest.

Three

Val was Owed an Explanation. Val was, after all, my best friend, and she'd presided over the development of my relationship with Art, usually by loudly disapproving of him at every turn. She'd said he was arrogant, spoilt, oversexed and shallow, and when proved resoundingly right she *hadn't* said 'I told you so'.

She'd seen our reconciliation, too. She'd been in McDonald's with me and cleared off to let Art and me talk. And she'd shown enormous self-restraint and only phoned three times since, trying to get hold of me.

Val was Owed. I went round to see her.

'You're *WHAT*??!'

'Val, don't get all self-righteous with me.'

'You're going out with him again. I don't believe it. All he has to do is wander in and say – Hey, sorry, I was a bit out of order then – and it's all kissy-kissy make up, everything forgiven.'

'No. *No*! Just listen to me, will you. I'm just saying how I *feel* about him ...'

'Oh, we all know how you *feel* about him. Your tongue hasn't been back in your mouth since you first clapped *eyes* on him. But he *lied* to you! He *used* you! He's a total *git*! And now you're just going to ...'

I buried my head in my arms on the table so I wouldn't have to hear. 'Val, I know everything you're saying. I do. But things are different now – he's different. We've really talked. We're so much closer ...'

'I see. So Wonderboy manages to string a few words together, and suddenly it's all all right. No – *don't* go on about how you understand him and how he has a permissive dad and everything. I just don't buy it.'

'But it really does explain –'

'It's actions that count, Coll. That's what you should judge people on. I don't go for this sympathy-for-the-psycho stuff. And anyway, understanding *why* he's a git doesn't make him *less* of one. You say he's changed but how do you *know* he's changed? You've only seen him once. Twice, then. *Big* deal.'

Listening to Val was exhausting. Being right gave her this terrible, loud energy. 'I'm just going to start seeing him again,' I mumbled. 'I'm going to see how it goes.'

'Oh, it'll *go* all right,' she snapped.

'It's better for a woman to regret something she's done,' I croaked, 'than something she hasn't done. That's an old quote.'

'In this context, it's also utter *crap*,' Val said. 'Who wrote it, anyway? Some bloody man, that's who. Art's great-grandfather, probably.'

I gave up.

Mum also had to Be Faced. Not a gentle prospect. She had this way of loudly overwhelming you with her point of view, however well prepared you were to defend yours. And Art wasn't a topic she exactly held back on. She was deeply prejudiced against men in general, and so far everything Art had done had only served to deepen those prejudices further. Still, I had a slight advantage with Mum, because she'd told Art where to find me. She'd brought us together again.

'RUBBISH,' she said indignantly. I did not bring you together. I simply gave out information. I never interfere in your private life.''

'Mum!! That is the most outrageous *lie* I've ever heard!'

She shrugged her broad shoulders. 'I only want what's good for you, Colette. If you can work things out with that-young-man, then I'll be happy for you. But BE CAREFUL! He's not to be trusted, I could see that from the start. He's been completely spoilt by his good looks, his money, that ridiculous, privileged school he goes to, his TOTAL LACK OF PARENTAL SUPERVISION! Don't pull that face at me. I just don't want to see you getting hurt. Not again. Not by someone like him. You're worth two of him, Colette. The concept of respect doesn't seem to EXIST for him – or his family. He comes from a background that's positively amoral – he's been allowed to do JUST what he wants. No wonder he behaved like he did. People are what they've been made, you know. You tell me it's different now, well, I hope so, for your sake, because if he ...'

'Mum,' I said, weakly, 'spare me. Please.'

'Everyone hates you,' I said to Art when I met up with him the next night.

'Great.'

'Do you care?'

'Not really. I care about what you think.'

'Well – I don't. Hate you I mean.'

'That's good,' he said, grinning, and he put a hand out to my hair, and I got hold of the lapels on his jacket, and soon we were kissing. Then we put our arms around each other and began to wander along, no idea where we were going.

'I had a real roasting from Val,' I said. 'And Mum *confined* herself to a half-hour lecture but I bet she's storing more up for later. What's your dad said?'

'About what?'

'About us getting back together again?'

Art turned to look at me. 'Why would I tell him? Christ, I haven't *seen* him all week.'

'Oh.' I pondered that fact for a moment. 'So where's he been?'

'I dunno. Probably running round after someone new.'

'God. Doesn't Fran *mind*?'

'She knew what he was like when she married him. She does her own thing too. She spends his money.'

'That is so *sad*.'

'That's survival.'

'Has he always been – like that?'

'No. He flipped when my mum died.' Art's voice had gone kind of monotone, and for a moment I thought he was going to leave it at that, but then he said, 'They were real close, and this – this thing, this cancer, just wiped her out. I mean – it happened so quickly – three months. He went mad. Right up to the end, he thought they'd save her.'

I tightened my arm round his waist, willing him to talk. 'How old were you?' I asked tentatively, 'when this ... happened?'

'Oh – I dunno. Twelve. He started going out, drinking. He'd stay out really late. He'd go away all weekend. He got tied up with woman after woman, none of them lasted more than a few weeks. I reckon he's scared to – you know, put it all on to one woman again.'

We walked on slowly, and I thought of Art at twelve, with both parents suddenly gone. 'So who was with you?' I asked.

'My aunt used to come round, make me meals and stuff. She had this crap theory about Dad dealing with his grief. All I knew was that these women were with him, when I wanted to be.'

'Oh, Art. That's awful, that's –'

He shrugged. 'It's in the past.'

And in you, I thought, and still so painful you can hardly bear to talk about it. We walked on and found a little, out-of-the-way pub. It was like we were fugitives, not wanting to bump into anyone we knew. We sat as close to each other as we could get in a corner seat, and I leant against his shoulder.

He's talking, I thought, he's finally talking. I've learnt more about him in the last ten minutes than in the whole time I've known him. That drama we went through, all that pain – it was worth it, to be close like this.

Art had got hold of my hand and was looking down at

it, all serious. Then he muttered 'Coll ... er ... d'you want to – would you like ...?' and fell silent.

For one crazy minute I thought he was going to ask me to marry him or something. Whatever it was sounded so important. 'Would you – will you come to the match on Saturday?' he finally said.

'Match? What match?'

'I'm playing. You know – rugby. It's the last match of the season. Will you come?'

I said yes, of course. I'd have said yes if he'd invited me to watch him watch paint drying. He started to talk about his team and how much he liked playing; after a minute or so I drifted off and didn't really hear what he was saying. I focused instead on the way all his attention was on me, on the way he stared into my eyes. I stared back, watching every move on his face, soaking up the enjoyment in his voice.

We left the pub soon afterwards and walked a long detour home, arms round each other. We passed a little alley shaded by a lanky tree, and kind of came to a stop. Then it seemed the most natural thing in the world to slide into the alley together.

Art leant back against the wall and said, 'Coll. Thank you for going out with me again. You are, aren't you? This isn't a one off?'

I laughed and put my arms around his neck, then I reached up and kissed him. We kissed slowly, him waiting for my lead, then me waiting for him, response on response on response. When we stopped I slid my hands down his chest and heard myself give this kind of mew of pleasure.

'What was that for?' he asked, grinning.

'What?'

'That *mmeeugh*. That moan. You sounded like someone off a phone sex line.'

'How would you know? D'you ring them up?'

He hugged me to him and breathed in this jokey-sultry voice, 'Coll, that was lust. Admit I drive you crazy.'

'Get lost,' I laughed. 'Come on, let's go.'

'Not yet,' he said, giving me a smouldering look from under his eyelashes. 'Please.'

I laughed again, and he kind of enveloped me, kissing me all the way down my neck, his hands working their way up inside my sweatshirt. Something inside my head told me to stop him, but I didn't.

18

Four

Val nearly fell off her chair laughing when I told her I was going to watch Art play rugby. 'What about your *pompoms*,' she gurgled hysterically.

'My *what*?' I snapped.

'Your pompoms. You'll need one for each hand, and a little short skirt, and then you shout ROO ROO WE love YOU – '

'Val – '

' – and then you stick your bum in the air and shove your head through your legs and shout, "Come on boys –nuffin to it! You can win – we've seen you do it!"'

'*Val* – do you want a smack in the *mouth*?'

'Sorry – sorry,' she gurgled. 'Hey – that was quite good, that rhyme.'

'No it wasn't. It was painful. And that's *cheerleading*. I am *not* going as a cheerleader!'

'Good as. You stand on the touchline watching an appalling game just 'cos Hunk Features is in it – that's cheerleading in my opinion. Worse than cheerleading. Not as much fun.'

'Val, shut up. I'm – interested, that's all.'

'Oh, *balls*. You are *not*. You know *nothing* about rugby.'

'I do.'

'OK. What's the scoring system?'

Val had me there, and she knew it. I hung my head, defeated. 'Oh, Val, I've *got* to go. He'd come and watch me.'

'*In what*?! You aren't in any teams. You hate competitive sport.'

'Oh, OK Val! But if you'd seen his face when he asked – it was like he was letting me in on this – special event – I mean, I felt *honoured* –'

Val had closed her eyes in despair. 'There's no hope for you, girl,' she said.

If Val had been scathing, Mum would be blistering, I was sure of that. But I was going to face it out. On Saturday afternoon I was sitting on the stairs pulling on my old DMs when she emerged from the kitchen and asked, 'Off on some hike, are you?'

I barely hesitated. 'I'm watching Art play rugby,' I muttered.

'RUGBY? Art plays rugby? Well – good for him.'

Sometimes I think if she lives to be a hundred that woman will never, ever stop surprising me.

'You like rugby?' I said, evenly.

'Good God, no. Dreadful game. But it's good for them. Young boys, I mean. Gets rid of some of their aggression.

Better to smash each other up on the field than run riot somewhere else. You see, Colette, MALE ENERGY has nowhere productive to go in the twentieth century. The sort of energy that was vital once to fight off marauders and kill mammoths – it has to be CHANNELLED, and rugby –'

'Mum – '

' – isn't such a bad way of doing it. They go on about skill and sportsmanship, but they really just want to be pelting down to the shoreline with their axes and horned helmets, ready to chop the invader to bits – '

'*MUM!!*'

'Yes?'

'Have you finished? I mean – where do you get this stuff from?'

She shrugged. 'I would have thought it was all pretty self-evident,' she said, and swept upstairs.

Five

Not long after that I heard a car horn outside, and I ran out. Art had made me swear to come out quickly so that he didn't have to come into contact with Mum.

He half-emerged from the back seat and said, 'Ready?' Then he let me in beside him.

He had this different feel to him – keyed up, cut off, focused. There were two other blokes in the car and it was full of the same energy. I had this sudden picture of them wearing Viking helmets and had to bite the inside of my cheek so I wouldn't laugh. 'Thanks a lot, Mum,' I thought. 'You've really helped.'

My feelings about going to this match were so mixed I couldn't begin to sort them out. I was pleased Art had asked me – really pleased. And I wanted to see him play, although I thought it might get a bit tedious. But Val and I had always been completely merciless towards the sort of girl who went along to things just because her boy-friend was involved. And we'd always taken the piss out of any form of macho behaviour. Now here I was doing a kind of double, duplicated about-turn ...

When we got to the sports ground, Art ushered me towards the edge of the field, where a few girls in posh anoraks were standing around, arms folded, chatting.

I'm a Supporting Girlfriend, I thought. Oh, the shame.

'Hey – Meg,' Art called out, and a dark-haired girl turned towards him.

'Hey, Ponso,' she replied.

'This, is Coll,' he said. I smiled, nervously.

'You've *never* bought your girlfriend to watch, have you?' she said, in a strong Welsh accent. 'That's a first.'

As I tried not to show the deep pleasure I felt on hearing this, she turned to me and said, 'He's a crap player. I don't know why they let him in the team.'

'Oh, piss off, Meg,' he said. 'Coll – I have to go.'

It didn't seem in order to kiss him goodbye. He ran off towards the club house.

'I don't know much about rugby, I'm afraid,' I muttered to Meg.

'Well – you can't know less than that lot,' she said, jerking her head towards the Supporting Girlfriends. 'It takes them half the match to work out who's playing which end.'

'Ah. Is Art really a crap player?'

'Nah. I was just giving him a bit of encouragement.'

More and more people were arriving and standing round the pitch. 'Good turnout,' said Meg, approvingly. Then there was a burst of clapping, and I looked up to see some huge blokes in blue tops run out onto the field.

Then a second lot in green tops ran out. The sound their boots made was weird – like fast marching. It felt like the start of a battle.

'God, look at the size of them,' I hissed. 'Half of them haven't got *necks*! Look at that ugly brute – '

'There's my brother!' said Meg fondly. I withdrew my pointing finger, hastily.

Art ran out last. 'What's he done to his *teeth*?' I wailed.

Megan turned to glare at me. 'Don't you know *anything*?' she said. 'That's a mouthguard. Only the ponsos wear them.'

The whistle went, and a player hoofed the ball into the air. Art leapt to get it, but so did someone else. There was a horrific thudding sound and the two of them crashed to the ground. 'Oн!' I wailed. Then Art got to his feet, and ran after the ball, but within minutes he'd crashed to the ground again, this time under a heap of thrashing bodies.

'Oн!' I wailed. 'He'll be hurt!'

Meg, laughing, explained the rudiments of the game, but I couldn't begin to take it in. The scoring system seemed totally unimportant next to the imminent likelihood of one of the players getting his head kicked off. I stood watching in fascination and horror, wringing my hands and whimpering 'Oh, no!' every time they all smashed into each other or Art hit the ground. It was all so fast, so fierce. I couldn't believe I'd expected to be bored. I was riveted.

Maybe this is where Art's rather casual attitude to sex comes from, I thought. If you're used to doing this with your body, maybe sex isn't such a big deal.

After half an hour or so the score was even: two penalties, one to each side. 'Half time soon,' said Meg, ruefully. 'No real action yet.'

I gawped at her. No *action*? Was she *blind*? 'I can't *believe* this,' I hissed. 'What a *stupid* game! Why don't they just forget the ball and beat each other to a pulp? How can they *do* that to themselves?'

'Don't be soft, girl,' Meg said.

Then, suddenly, Meg's brother made a break from the scrum of players, clutching the ball. He launched himself forward and bulled through two blokes, then a third brought him down. He threw the ball out as he fell, and Art caught it. Then Art was running, really fast, racing for the line, as everyone charged towards him.

'*GO!! GO!!*' I heard myself screaming.

'*RUN!*' yelled Meg.

Someone came from his right, but he smashed through and ran, pelting over the line as two other players hurled themselves at him. They all crashed down together.

'Did he *do* it?' I yelled at Meg through all the cheering.

'Course he bloody did!' she yelled back. Then we jumped up and down and cheered so loudly that the Supporting Girlfriends looked over at us, scandalised.

On the pitch, the players were far more restrained. Art ran back into the centre, with only two slaps on the shoulder for congratulation.

'Well done, Ponso!' shouted Meg. He looked towards me and grinned, and I smiled back. I could feel myself melting at the delight on his face.

'Don't go getting all proud of him,' Meg said. 'The game isn't over yet.'

'I don't think I can take much more,' I whimpered. 'Do you always come and watch your brother?'

She nodded. 'When I haven't got a match on myself.'

*

25

The second half was even wilder. There were three more penalties, two in the other team's favour – and then they got a try. A scrambled, mean little try compared to the one Art had got, I thought – but a try nonetheless. The opponents were ahead.

Meg started really bellowing at our players, berating them, encouraging them. They were playing faster and faster, crashing up and down the field in a welter of mud.

'We're into injury time!' said Meg despairingly. I saw Art disappear under a pile of bodies again, then someone chucked out the ball, and a guy from Art's team caught it and the players fanned out and moved forward fast, passing the ball back, back, back. Then one of them made a bolt for it and ran, swerving through the opposition, and soared forward – over the line.

Uproar.

With a perfect kick, the try was 'converted'. There was a bit more shambling about, and then the final whistle went.

We'd won.

I staggered into the club room with an ecstatic Meg, who was ranting on about the other team's lack of tackling commitment. I was dazed. That was some alien spectacle, I thought. Barbaric. Brilliant. Men really are from another planet.

Art had looked so good when he'd run full out, though – when he'd scored the try. I'd never seen him that committed, that reckless. He'd looked unbeatable. Watch it, Coll, I thought sternly. You're coming over all quivery.

All the spectators were wandering into the bar, chatting and laughing. Huge plates of filled rolls and fruit cake were carried in and dumped on tables. Meg got me a drink. Then there was a commotion at the far end and both the teams filed in through the doors, all showered and changed, pushing each other about and laughing and calling out to people. Everyone started clapping again, shouting congratulations.

I felt really excited. I started craning round everyone, trying to see Art. Meg headed purposefully off into the centre of the players, and I followed. Then I saw Art, coming straight towards me. His hair was all wet and brushed back, he had a big cut over his eyebrow, and a bruise on his cheekbone. I wanted to put my arms round him so badly I could feel my breathing going funny.

'Hey, Coll,' he said.

'You won,' I breathed. 'That was just amazing, it was – '

'Your girlfriend was so worried about you getting your soft face smashed in she could barely stand upright,' interrupted Meg, happily. 'You were really showing off out there.'

'What did you think of it?' Art said to me.

'It was – I thought it was – '

'Anyone could've got that try, the way I set it up,' put in Meg's brother, and Art shoved him backwards, swearing and laughing, and Meg said, 'You all played like a load of girls' blouses to start off with,' and then a kind of uproar took over, everyone joking and celebrating.

I didn't know what to say, what to do. I couldn't be part of it, I didn't have the right words. All I wanted to do was wrap myself round Art, but I didn't. There was lots of male-to-male touching, but nothing going on between the sexes. So I just leaned closer and closer to him as the noise level rose until he put his arm round me

27

and said, 'Help me get the next round in?'

'Are you OK?' I asked, when we were alone by the bar. 'Really? You looked like you were being mashed out there.'

'I'm fine.'

'Doesn't it *hurt*?'

'I'll be stiff tomorrow. What did you think of the game?'

'Art – I was gobsmacked. I mean – it was astonishing. I half think you're a hero and I half think you're insane.'

'Stick with the first half,' he said cockily, as we carried the drinks back to the others. 'I'm one hell of a hero.' Meg's brother overheard him say this, unfortunately, and a lot of abuse and joking followed. As it all died down Art and I found ourselves gradually moving to the edge of the group. We stood side by drinking, not talking, then Art got hold of my hand and towed me towards the door.

'I want to show you something,' he said. 'It'll crease you up.'

We clattered up the stairs hand in hand and went into a large room with a big central table and lots of chrome and leather chairs. 'This is the committee room,' Art explained. 'Go and have a look at that wall.'

I wandered across. Rows of long, framed photographs filled the far wall. Ranks and ranks of school rugby teams, long shorts in the fifties, long hair in the seventies, all sitting in the same way, with crossed arms and determined faces. 'You're right,' I said, as I moved along gazing at them, 'these are hilarious.' I'd started to get the giggles. Art came up close behind me and put his arms round my waist, nuzzling his face into my hair, and the real reason for coming to this empty room dawned on me.

'Where's yours?' I asked. 'Your team photograph? I bet that's a real scream.'

'Not up yet,' he said. 'Not good enough yet.'

I turned my head and rubbed my cheek against his mouth, and he moved his hands up to my breasts. I twisted round inside his arms, facing him. 'Yes you are good enough,' I said. 'I still can't get over how hard you played out there.' I reached up and stroked the skin near the cut on his eyebrow.

Art pulled my hand from his face, and started kissing me, holding me close. 'Art,' I murmured, 'someone could come in.'

'D'you want to hide then?'

'Where?'

He jerked his head towards a huge leather sofa in the corner, high as a barricade. 'Behind that?'

We walked over silently and sat down behind the sofa a bit awkwardly, a bit stupidly, then Art got hold of me and we slithered to the carpet, lying side by side, and started really kissing, making up for all the time in the bar when we'd only been able to look at each other. Then he moved half on top of me, stroking my hair, my neck, my breasts, running his hand right down my body, then up again, snaking his fingers down the waistband of my jeans. I could hear his breathing, faster and faster, and I suddenly had this flashback to the last time we'd petted like this, in the long grass in the garden at his dad's cottage, two weeks ago, before everything had been blown apart.

'What's wrong?' Art said.

'What d'you mean?'

'You've gone all – it's like you've turned off.'

'I was just – I was thinking about that time at the cottage.'

'Oh, God.' He rolled away and sat up. 'I'm sorry, Coll.'

'No,' I said, 'it's not that. Jesus, if you knew what I – ' Then I threw myself on him and kissed him. It's different now, completely different, I said to myself fiercely. I'm not some kind of victim, I've *chosen*. I undid his shirt, and kissed him all over his chest, then in some sort of desperation, I undid his jeans, and he helped me, like he'd helped me that night in the garden.

'Coll,' he groaned, after a while. 'Coll, stop. We'd better go.'

'Afraid you'll get kicked off the team?' I murmured, 'if we're caught here?'

'Something like that,' he muttered, smiling.

I was kind of relieved when we stood up to go, when we went down the stairs together, hand in hand. No one in the bar seemed to have missed us – everyone was in the process of leaving. Art's mate who'd stayed self-righteously sober gave us a lift home and dropped us off at the end of my road. We took two steps towards my house, then he stopped, and started kissing again. We both knew that it meant a lot, what had happened in the empty committee-room, and me going to watch him play, see another side of him, that meant a lot too, but neither of us was going to say anything about it.

Well, we didn't need to.

Six

Art and I managed to meet several times over the next two weeks. He wouldn't come to my house because he was terrified of Mum, and I wouldn't go to his house because the very thought of seeing his dad again made me shrivel up with embarrassment. But we found places to meet.

Sometimes it felt weird — like having a secret liaison and I wished we weren't so secretive, so cut off from everyone. But most of the time it felt wonderful. The energy between us growing all the time. It was in everything we did, it coloured everything we said. It was like a hunger, finding places to be undisturbed, waiting for it to get dark on the streets.

Art was still talking, too. Not so much about personal stuff; not about me and him. That incredible openness between us when we'd first got back together had closed down a bit. Inevitable, I suppose. The rawness heals over, and you get back to everyday stuff. You put up defences. You can't live through every hour as though you're on the brink of something. Which is a shame in a way.

But even if he wasn't telling me what he felt about me, he was letting me into his mind much more. He had this stark view of the world that I found half-exhilarating, half-terrifying, all about being alone, depending on no one, being free. Every time we made a connection, every time we collided on the same wavelength, it was thrilling. He also had an incredibly evil sense of humour – he was amazed that I liked it, he said no other girl ever had. And whenever I made *him* laugh, I felt a huge sense of achievement.

I was besotted with him. I couldn't drag my eyes away from him when we were together, and when I was alone, I thought about him all the time. It scared me sometimes, because I still didn't feel sure of him, nothing like; but there was no way I wanted it to stop.

In the background, Mum and Val were like two grim guardians of my well-being. All the time I felt them watching me, and I felt their concern and disapproval, restrained only with difficulty.

Mum confined herself to long, meaningful looks whenever she caught me whispering into the phone or coming home very late after swimming on Thursday or going out of the house without explanation. Her opinion of Art was like a monolith on the landscape. Silent but massive, and always in your line of vision.

Val was a bit more verbal. She'd say sneery things like, 'Looking good, Coll. Wonderboy must have been *particularly* wonderful last night' and 'Coming out with us Friday? Oh, no stupid question, right? You have to go and worship at Hunk Features' feet.' She'd tell me all about her relationship with Greg, too; how caring and committed and responsible and totally unlike Art he was. Well, I knew all about that because I'd sort of gone out with him too at one time, but I let her get away with it all, because it was easier than fighting back.

I knew that one day we'd all have to work it out, and come into each others' lives again, but for the time being it suited me fine. All I was really interested in was what was happening between Art and me. I didn't care about other people fitting into it.

One gloomy Sunday, Art and I spent two hours just wandering about, having this great discussion about the lies people live by, the fake structures they build up. We really got into it. He accused me of being too positive about people; I accused him of being a cynic. Then we went into a little café and continued to fight over coffee and rolls. When we'd paid and walked outside, Art suddenly stopped and put his arms round me. 'I really like arguing with you, Coll,' he said. 'It's great.'

I laughed and hugged him back, trying not to show how pleased I was. 'I'm not used to *talking* to people I fancy,' he went on.

'Yeah, well, that's where you've missed out,' I said. 'This male thing you have of putting everything in boxes –'

'Oh, no. Not another bloody lecture.'

'I mean – it's all connected. Talking's brought us closer, and now I ... I ... '

He tightened his hold on me. 'Now you *what*?'

I didn't answer, and he said, 'I think ... your ideas are right. You know – what you said about getting close to someone before you shag them?'

33

'I am right. And do *try* not to call it shagging, you yob.'

'And we're close now. You just said we were.'

I laughed and tried to push him away, but he stayed close. Then I took a deep breath and said, 'I used to have this theory about holistic sex.'

'*What?* I've heard of most things, but ... '

'Holistic sex means everything's involved – mind, body, spirit, emotions. When you both know every side of each other – you can begin to fuse. Then sex is really something. I imagine.'

'Christ, you and your words.'

'It's got to be special. Transforming.'

'Those are huge demands. I'll never live up to it. I mean – if I – if we – '

I laughed. 'You don't have to. That's the point. When you're close – it's supposed to just happen.'

'Holistic sex,' he repeated. 'I like that. I've missed out on all that. When you said it was like a sport to me, you were right. I'd got good, too.'

'Don't boast. It's pathetic. And I'm sure you're Olympic standard. But in terms of *holistic* sex, you're as much of a virgin as I am.'

That made him really laugh. And then we started making love. Not the whole way, because we were standing in the street, but it was making love all the same.

Making love, not the whole way. We did an awful lot of that over those few weeks, whenever we had any privacy, and sometimes when we didn't. I knew now that Mum was right, with her view that straight-away sex is as grim as a Victorian wedding night. You can't jump from kissing to sex and expect it to be good. You've got to work up to it, you've got to feel ready.

And now I felt so ready I was approaching meltdown. Art was very careful not to push it, but I think we both knew we'd sleep together sometime soon.

Seven

For Art and his friends, one year ahead of me and my friends, it was the year of Eighteenth Birthday Celebrations. Kids whose parents hadn't given them a party since there was jelly and icecream on the menu were suddenly booking halls, ordering helium balloons and arguing about elderly relatives being included on the guest list. Or saying: Look, you know it's been a tight year – why don't you just take some friends out for a pizza?

Being eighteen was a Big Deal.

Saturday night, in the pub, Art pulled a scrunched up bit of card out of his back pocket and handed it to me. It said, 'Miss Stephanie Clancey requests the pleasure of Art Johnson (and guest) on the occasion of her 18th Birthday party on Saturday 3 May.'

'Want to be my guest?' he said. 'You're in brackets.'

'Flattering. Yes please. Art – look what you've done to

36

this invite. It's really posh and you've wrecked it. You're meant to prop it on the mantelpiece.'

'Why?'

'You just are. Who's Stephanie?'

'Oh – someone I used to … '

'Not another of your exes. I'm not going if she is.'

'No, I swear. Just a friend. Not even a friend. But – '

'What?'

'Well – there'll be someone there I could do without seeing.'

'Oh *yes*? And who's *she*?'

'He. Joe. I think – maybe we'll give the party a miss.'

'Art – tell me the story. Who is he?'

He grimaced. 'He used to be a really good mate. But we fell out. It was really stupid.'

'Don't tell me. You got off with his girlfriend or something?'

There was a long, long pause, and I said, 'Oh, God, Art. You're appalling.'

'Why do you assume it was *me*?'

'OK, what happened?'

'I … His girlfriend got off with me – '

'ART– !!'

'She was a *cow*. I don't know why I went along with it.'

'You shit. Your best mate.'

'I tried phoning him. He wouldn't speak to me. He really liked her. I told him I did him a favour … '

'Oh, please – '

' … showing him what she was like.'

'No wonder he wouldn't speak to you. Whatever made you *do* it?'

'It was *her*. I was drunk. And she really came on to me.'

'You know, Art, one day you're going to have to start taking responsibility for what you do. You can't keep blaming your dad, or drink, or girls going mad over you ...' I picked up my glass, self-righteously, and added, 'Maybe you can patch things up with him at the party.'

'I don't think so. He told me just thinking about me made him want to vomit.'

I laughed. 'He sounds OK. Maybe he'll try and get off with me. As revenge for you getting off with his girlfriend.'

Art looked at me. 'He'd like you,' he said.

When we were kissing good night, Art said, 'Why don't you come round to my place tomorrow?'

'Because I'd sooner have my legs chopped off, that's why.'

'You wouldn't have to see the old man.'

'Yeah, but I might bump into him. I can just imagine his *face*, and him saying, "Hello there, last representative of the Protected Species Virgin- "'

'He doesn't talk like that. No one does, except in your warped mind. And anyway,' he added, tightening his clinch on me, 'you're an Endangered Species now.'

'Oh, *smooth*! Don't make me puke.'

'Come on, Coll. He doesn't matter. We could go straight up to my room.'

'No way,' I said.

I worried myself silly about what to wear to the posh party. By the look of the scrolls and silver on the invitation, everyone would be in tiaras at the very least. In the end I blew just about all my money on a short, plain aubergine-coloured dress that 'showed off my athletic figure' according to Mum. I thought if I threw my hair about over it and wore my three big silver rings I'd look smart enough.

'Let's meet at seven,' said Art. 'We can go via the pub. I'm going to need a drink before this one.'

'OK. Come and pick me up then.'

Art paled. 'Come and pick you *up*? At your *house*?'

'Yes.'

'But I'll see your mum.'

'So?'

'She'll murder me.'

'No, she won't. Anyway, you were going on about me coming round to your house. Why can't you come to mine?'

'Because your mum is ... your *mum* is ... '

'Look, Art – we're going out again. You're going to have to face her one day.'

'Oh, God,' he said, sounding so piteous that I nearly weakened.

But only nearly.

'We've been acting like fugitives, Art,' I said, firmly. 'Creeping around, scared to phone each other up even. We've got to get normalised. We've got to face them, show them we're back together. Look – you come to my house, then I'll come to yours. That's a deal.'

When the doorbell went at ten past seven on Saturday night, I started to run downstairs, and then I stopped. Something wicked and wild had got into me, and it felt great. I sat down where I was on the stairs, which was an act of extreme cruelty, because it left Mum to open the front door to Art.

You could positively feel the negative shock waves when she did. I heard her direct him icily into the kitchen. Then I crept downstairs to eavesdrop. Before I reached the bottom, the doorbell went again. I retreated up to the bend in the stairs and watched three of Mum's friends troop in.

Mum's friends are much gentler than her but, like her, they're pretty anti-male. They like to get together regularly and listen to Mum slagging off the men in their lives.

It was perfect timing.

Everyone disappeared into the kitchen and I sped silently downstairs again and hid outside the door. I heard Mum introduce Art in barely concealed tones of disgust. Then I could hear them all gather round Art, bleating at him.

It was the wolf thrown to the sheep. I could picture him, choking and suffocating, in their midst.

'Coll's boyfriend? – but I thought that was all over ...'

'Keep up, Clare – that was weeks ago! They're back together now. APPARENTLY.'

'Oh, well, as long as Coll's happy.'

'I hope so. I VERY MUCH hope so.'

'She's such a bright girl. How's the A level course?'

'Oh, she's made a good start. I'm sure she'll do fine. As long as she doesn't get DISTRACTED.'

'Where is Coll? Making herself look beautiful?'

'God, the hours I used to spend getting ready to go out with some man. Oh, well. She'll learn men aren't worth it.'

'So where are you off to, young man? A party?'

'Eighteenth? How lovely!'

'Lovely? I wouldn't be eighteen again. Worst time of my life. If I knew then what I know now ... '

'Oh, it *is* lovely. And Coll's lovely too. So fit. All that swimming and biking she does ... '

'Are you into all that physical stuff, too, Art? Like Coll?'

That last question nearly finished me off. As I gasped silently for breath, the kitchen door burst open and Art burst out and got me in a double armlock. I started to shriek with laughter. Then he wrestled me out of the front door, slamming it behind us.

'You *cow*!' he said. 'You absolute *cow*!'

'Oh, God, that was priceless! That was brilliant!'

'How could you do that to me? You *wait*. You just *wait*.'

'What did Mum say to you?'

'Nothing. She didn't need to. You should have seen the way she *looked* at me. Like I was something disgusting she'd just stepped in – and who were those *women*? They kept staring me up and down, and *questioning* me ... '

'Oh, I love it. I *love* it!'

'You're dead, Coll. Good as dead. I said I'd come to your house, not face a *tribunal*.'

'I just wish I could've been in there with you,' I crowed, 'and seen your face.'

'You still hate me, don't you? You must do. What was that, some kind of *test*?'

'I'm sorry, I'm sorry,' I gurgled. 'But anyway, you passed.'

We staggered off to the pub, and after a while, Art saw the funny side, too. Then he spent a long time outlining how he was going to get back at me. He reckoned he'd paid his side of the bargain so many times over that nothing I could ever do would make up for it. We were having such a good time we almost forgot about the posh party, and left the pub in a mad rush.

Art found the house, huge and intimidating behind its wrought iron gates. As he knocked on the door I suddenly had an attack of nerves. It was OK for Art – he was used to wealth, grandeur and the high life. But I wasn't. 'Do I look all right?' I hissed. Spontaneous compliments weren't exactly Art's thing – you had to ask.

'Terrific,' he said, 'Really sexy. Why are we going to this stupid party anyway ... ?'

The door had swung open and a woman with a gold dress and steel eyes was glaring at us. Then she suddenly smiled. 'I know *you*!' she barked. 'You're Ian's boy, aren't you! Come on in!'

We stumbled over the threshold and Art muttered, 'This is Colette,' just too quiet for the woman to hear. She disappeared through a doorway carolling, 'Stephanie! More guests, darling!'

This was a formal affair, all right. More like a wedding than a birthday party. I felt quite intimidated as I looked around me. Three girls in bright, flouncy frocks emerged and surrounded Art, waving their arms about and planting kisses on his face.

'Oh, Arty,' cooed one of them, 'I'm so glad you came!'

Arty, I thought. Give me strength. They bore him like a trophy into the huge party room, and I followed. A tray of fruit punch sailed past my nose, too fast for me to grab one. None of the girls took any notice of me. Maybe they thought I was a waitress. I suppose I was dressed a bit like one, compared to them. Then more guests were announced, and the welcoming committee rushed off, and Art and I melted towards the corner of the room.

'How you doing, *Arty*,' I said. 'They practically ate you just then.'

'You're just jealous,' he replied, preening.

'Don't flatter yourself. I hate all that kissy-kissy stuff – it makes me want to – ' but my next words disappeared into the folds of a tartan waistcoat.

'Colette!' I heard. 'Well, well!' It was Art's obnoxious non-friend Mark, clasping me to his breast. 'Art said you were *history*!'

Tactful as ever, I thought, as I shoved him backwards.

'Back together again, ay?' he said. 'What happened?'

'We just couldn't keep apart, Mark,' Art said drily. 'You know how it is.'

'Oh, absolutely,' gurgled Mark. 'Don't I just.' And he turned and leered at Sally, who was walking over to join us. Sally was Mark's girlfriend; she was also one of Art's exes. You didn't need to be psychic to see that she'd like those two roles reversed. She ignored Mark and started winding herself like a barracuda round Art, cooing, 'It's lovely to *see* you! Oh—hi, Colette. Art – how *are* you? We've *missed* you! Joe's here. Did you know?'

Art scanned the room anxiously and I asked, 'Which one's Joe?'

'There,' said Mark, pointing. 'In the brown jacket. Shall I call him over here ... ?'

'Leave it,' muttered Art. 'Let's get a drink.' And he started to walk off.

'Aren't you going to speak to him at all?' I hissed, following.

'Leave it,' he repeated.

At the drinks table, Art was immediately surrounded

by people yelping 'Where have you *been*?' and 'We haven't seen you for ages!' Some fun party this is going to be, I thought sourly. Art wasn't exactly hating all the attention, either. He kept kind of shaking back his hair and smirking. After a few more minutes I was so fed up I swallowed the rest of my drink and stalked off to find the bog. He can come and find me, I thought – if he ever notices I've gone missing.

I spent far longer in the bathroom than I needed, fluffing out my hair and putting on two lots of lipstick. Then I went slowly back downstairs. Art was still by the drinks table, in among a crowd of people. 'You git,' I thought. I was damned if I was going to go over there and tug at his sleeve. I stood against the wall, scowling, looking at all the overdressed people, feeling totally out of it. Then another tray of fruit punch went past and this time my grab was successful.

You git, Art, I thought again. Come and find me, can't you? I could feel little pricklings of hurt that he was ignoring me like that. I told myself to get realistic – he wasn't the sort to stay welded to your side all evening, and I wasn't the sort that needed looking after. But even so, you'd think he'd be a bit more concerned about how I was, considering I didn't know anyone here, and you'd think he'd *want* to be with me ... I watched as Sally insinuated her way to his side again and started laughing hysterically at something he'd said, and I had all these depressing thoughts about how weird it was that someone as lush as Art wanted to be with someone as ordinary as me, thoughts I hadn't had once since we'd got back together again.

I wandered round the room feeling worse and worse,

then I went into the big conservatory at the back of the house. The guy in the brown jacket was there, alone, staring out into the garden. I walked over to him.

'You're Joe, aren't you?' I said.

Eight

Joe turned round to face me. 'Yes,' he said, doubtfully. He had a good face – not exactly handsome, but interesting. He was dark, like Art, but he looked older. And softer, somehow.

'You know Art Johnson?' I went on.

'Should I know *you*?' he asked, but not nastily.

'No. Mark pointed you out – you know, that cretin with – '

He smiled. 'I know Mark.'

'Anyway. I'm Colette. I'm going out with Art.'

His eyebrows went up, and I added, 'He told me about the row you had.'

I don't know what had got into me. The fruit punch, probably. I'm not usually this pushy.

'Where is he?' said Joe.

'Over there,' I said, indicating. 'In that group.'

46

Joe stared. 'Feeding his ego again. Smooth bastard.'

I laughed, taken aback, and then he laughed too and said, 'How can you stand going out with him?'

'Well – I'm not sure I can, yet.'

'What did he tell you about the row?'

'That it was over a girl – and it was more her fault than his.'

He turned away, and looked out at the garden. 'I couldn't get over him, doing that,' he said.

'I don't blame you,' I said, with feeling.

He looked round at me. 'Has he sent you over to talk to me?'

'*No* way. When he first saw you, he went off in the opposite direction.'

'So,' he said, leaning back against the glass wall. 'What's the big attraction with Art? Same thing that attracts everyone else?'

I shrugged. 'Yes. And more.'

'Well – good luck. Maybe you'll last longer than all the others.'

'Thanks,' I said, ignoring the sarcasm. 'We've already split up once. Everyone thinks I'm mad to get involved again ... ' and I found myself launching into the whole story of our bust up. Joe listened, putting the odd question, adding his point of view, laughing.

We'd skipped all the usual preliminary sounding out you do with someone you've just met. We had being mistreated by Art in common, and between us we really worked him over.

Joe was great to talk to. He wasn't afraid to come out with theories and ideas, not like most blokes are. He said one of the things he'd liked about Art was the way he saw through the bullshit in life. And he liked his reckless side, although that caused lots of problems. I was plugging him as hard as I could for insights, details, anything, when I saw him glance up, startled. Art had come into the conservatory. And he looked wild.

'What's going on?' he said. 'What the hell are you doing?'

'I'm talking to your friend,' I answered loudly. 'And if you have a problem with that, I suggest you go off somewhere and take a long look at yourself.'

Then I swept out of the conservatory door into the garden.

I swept round a corner then collapsed back against a wall, heart pounding. Inside my head, I replayed my parting words and wished I'd said something that had sounded as important but actually made sense.

I waited for Art to come out after me, but he didn't. I waited to hear sounds of a fistfight in the conservatory, but I couldn't. Not even raised voices.

It was all a bit of an anti-climax.

After a while I skulked round the outside of the house and came back in through the kitchen. The music had been turned up in the main room now, and there was some dancing going on. Flattening myself against the wall to avoid the flailing arms, I skirted towards the conservatory. Joe and Art were still in there, leaning back against a window, side by side. They both had their arms folded; they both stared at a point just in front of their feet. I think some form of communication was going on, but it was difficult to be sure.

'Now *you* look like the kind of girl who can dance!'

I turned irritably, to face a man of about fifty. Oh, shit.

The birthday girl's dad, probably. I had to be polite.

'Come on, I want to jive,' the man repeated plaintively. 'None of these kids know how to dance.'

Then he seized my hand and pulled me into the room, saying, 'I'm Don. Old family friend. I'll show you the steps.'

I was cringing as he towed me along, but the thing is, I did know how to jive, a bit. My Uncle Max had taught me. He'd insisted jiving was a life-skill.

Don went over to the music centre and switched CDS. None of the dancers seemed to mind. Most of them probably didn't even notice. Then he pulled me into an empty space and said, 'GO!'

No sense in being half-hearted about this, I thought – and I went.

He was a terrific dancer. Far better than Uncle Max. I only knew the basics, but with him leading, I felt like a pro. 'Go!' he kept saying. 'You're good!'

I started laughing, but I kept dancing. Another couple had stopped to watch us, leaving a bigger space. Then the music changed, and Don went into something more complicated. I struggled to keep up with him, spun away from his hand and back again. I was having a ball.

'Bugger off, young man,' Don suddenly said. 'Find your own partner.'

I looked up. Art was looking straight at me, a bit ironic and a bit impressed.

'Don't stop!' Don commanded, breathlessly. 'Tell that yob to go away!' And he spun me off again.

After a few more minutes there was a squawk from the sound system, and something slow came on. 'Oh, blast it,' said Don, as we wavered and stood still. He let go of my hand, turned on Art and said, 'Are you responsible for this, young man?'

Art didn't answer. He just moved in between us and put his arms round me, and I put my arms round him, trying not to go completely rigid with pleasure, and we danced.

'About *time*,' I said, after a minute or so. 'I was beginning to think I'd come to this bash on my own.'

'Christ, Coll, you were the one who went off.'

'Only because you were surrounded by exes.'

'What, Sally? Do me a favour. Don't you think I'm romantic, getting them to put a slow one on?'

'*Dead* romantic.'

'God, Coll, you're really hot. You're sweating.'

'Thanks a lot. Jiving does that to you.'

'You were good.'

'Thanks. Where's Joe?'

'Over there. They're dishing up some food. D'you want some?'

'And have you made up now?' I persisted.

'Sort of.'

'What did you talk about? When I left?'

'Coll – if you're trying to take the credit for this ...'

'Too right I am! If it hadn't been for me – '

'Oh, God. You're unbearable, you know that?'

'– you would have avoided him all evening.'

Art stood still and said, 'OK. What were *you* talking to him about.'

'That,' I answered, 'is my business.'

We pushed our way over to get some food. The table was groaning with scrumptious stuff. Stephanie's mum had done her proud.

'Here you are, star,' Art said, handing me a plate. 'Pile it up.' And we started dishing bits of food onto each others' plates, giggling like kids. I could feel this kind of delicious, grudging admiration from Art, which I put down to the fact that, rather than hang around and watch him getting gooed over, I'd gone off and found some interesting things to do on my own. Like jiving and cross-examining his ex-best friend. To tell the truth, I was feeling pretty chuffed with myself.

'Are you having an eighteenth party?' I asked Art, as we chewed.

'Not if I can help it. I had a sixteenth one. It was horrific. Fran did it. All spangly and balloons and things. I got really drunk and nearly got in a fist fight with my old man and then I threw up.'

'Lovely. And — '

'I snogged nearly everyone in the room.'

'Was that after or before you threw up?'

While we were laughing, Joe appeared at Art's side. 'I'm off now,' he announced.

'OK,' said Art.

'I'll see you.'

'Yeah.'

Reconciliation, male-style, I thought. You can't beat it for brevity.

We took our plates, sat on the floor in the corner, snuggled up against each other and ate. It was so good, just to be close to him, knowing he didn't want to be anywhere else either.

Stephanie was screaming happily over a huge pink cake that was being wheeled in, candles blazing. 'I want some of that,' Art said.

'Oh, gross.'

'Why doesn't she get on with it and cut it up?'

'Because she's spinning out the ritual. That cake is a symbol of her eighteen years.'

'Great symbol. A pink cake.'

'Did you get her a present?'

Art shrugged. 'Should I have done?'

'Well – yes. But you let her snog you. That has to be enough for any girl.'

He put his arm round me. 'We didn't *snog*,' he said.

'Good as. It's really bad manners to take someone to a party and then ... disappear under a pile of girls. I'm still pissed off with you.'

'Joe said I didn't deserve you.'

I brightened. 'He did?'

'Don't get excited. He doesn't think I deserve anyone.'

'Oh.'

'But he did like you. He said he'd phone me in a couple of weeks – so we can go out for a drink.'

'Oh, Art, great. That's *great*.'

Art turned to look at me, eyes all soft, and just then the raucous strains of 'Happy Birthday' filled the air. Stephanie had finally blown her candles out. 'Come on, let's get out of here,' Art grimaced. 'Let's go into the garden.'

No one noticed us dump our plates and leave. The lights from the conservatory flooded the lawn near the house, and round the edge there were garden candles on poles. As we walked away from the house, I realised there was another light. The moon was almost full.

'Look at that,' said Art. 'Don't start sprouting teeth and claws, Coll.'

'Werewolves are always men,' I said. 'Women make better vampires. God, how rich *is* Stephanie?'

The garden seemed to go on for ever. We wandered along, hand in hand, and I felt on such a high that I admitted to Art how intimidated I'd been when we'd first arrived.

He looked down at me, puzzled. 'You? Intimidated? What by?'

'You know – it's so posh. All the ... *conspicuous consumption*.'

We passed a fake Greek statue in a shrubbery, and Art laughed. 'You've got to be joking. It's all crap.'

'Yeah, but expensive crap,' I said, 'Look – they've even got a little summerhouse.'

We went over to inspect it. Art ducked his head and went inside, and I followed. Cane garden furniture was crowded in the middle of the floor, deck-chairs and umbrellas were stacked round the sides, and the moon shone through the open door.

Art threw himself down on the cane couch and pummelled the cushions. 'No mice,' he announced. 'No bugs, even. Come on, Coll.' He looked at me, waiting.

Why do people always describe moonlight as cold? It was alive; it was like something alive in the little wooden house with us, silvery, beautiful. I could feel it right through me.

The couch was just big enough for us to lie down together, me half on top of Art. The moon lit up our arms as we wrapped them round each other, but our faces were in darkness. And this time once we'd started kissing I knew I wanted more, right away I wanted more.

We coiled round each other, my mouth on his neck,

his on my face, kissing each other, touching each other, writhing, moving, all the time moving as if we'd destroy something if we stopped. And I felt so powerful. I was so far from being manoeuvred, manipulated. I was keeping pace.

'Coll,' he muttered, as we got wilder, 'is this – do you ...?'

I didn't answer. His hand moved down the back of my legs, moved to the front, and we were so near to it, so near to making love, and I wanted to go on, on, over the edge, but something pulled me back, something stopped me. I could hear him breathing fast, uncertain, and then we both heard a shout of shrill laughter from near the house.

We rocked each other, slowly, gently, and then we kissed. We both knew we wouldn't make love properly, not that night.

The moon shifted its light and left the summerhouse dark. Soon afterwards we went back into the house to find the party breaking up, and we went through the motions of saying goodbye and thank you. Stephanie insisted on presenting us both with a squashy slab of pink cake in a silver napkin. 'I couldn't see you *anywhere* when I was handing it round,' she said pointedly, 'you've *got* to have some.'

Then we escaped onto the doorstep, and down the drive. Outside the gates I stopped for a minute and looked up at the great pale disc of the moon. Art put his arm round me and looked up too, then he suddenly let out a howl like a wolf.

'Shut *up*,' I snapped. 'You nearly deafened me.'

'Sorry. Come on. Let's go.'

We wandered home, eating Stephanie's cake. 'I'm

going to be sick,' announced Art, pulling off a large strip of icing with his teeth and swallowing it.

'Chuck it away then.'

'Just one more bit. *Uurggh.*'

'Art,' I said, dumping the rest of my cake in a bin as we passed, 'when did you –? You know. Lose your virginity.'

He laughed. 'I was – it was just before my fifteenth birthday.'

'Oh, yuch. Who with?'

'Well – it was one of Fran's parties. Lots of people stayed over, and one of the guests took a fancy to me and – well, I was supposed to let her have my room, but I stayed in it too.'

I stared at him in absolute amazement. 'You mean one of *Fran's* friends?'

'No, one of Dad's.'

'Oh, *God.* That's even *worse.*'

'She was a lot younger than him. Someone he worked with. What are you looking so disgusted about? It was fantastic. For a fourteen-year-old.'

'If that happened to a *girl* – '

'The guy could get prosecuted. Yeah, I know.'

'And did you like her? The woman?'

'She laid me. Of course I liked her.'

'But what happened the next *day*?'

'She left really early. I think she was embarrassed.'

'Yeah. When she woke up and saw your cowboy outfit and Lego and – *God.* Did your Dad know what had happened?'

'Dunno. Think so. I'd just got kicked out from boarding school and I'd – '

'I didn't know you'd gone to boarding school.'

'I got sent off when I was thirteen. I was a real little shit when Dad got married – I gave Fran a really hard time. They'd both had a gutful.'

'And what did you get kicked out of school for?'

'Oh, I dunno. Dope. Truancy.'

'Sex orgies.'

'No, they came later,' he said sarcastically.

'Not much later.'

'Anyway, when I got back home it was like Dad had decided I'd grown up. He didn't care what I got up to.' Art stopped walking, turned to me, and said, 'Tomorrow. Your side of the bargain. I survived your place – *just* – now you've got to come round to mine. Only, because I'm not a raving sadist, *you* won't have to see anyone. Just me.'

I took a deep breath. 'Look Art – your dad might not care what you do in your room but there is *no* way ...'

'I understand, I understand. You're just visiting. We'll play chess or something.'

'OK. If I get there at ... at eleven, you promise you'll be the one to open the door?'

'Promise.'

'I don't trust you. You'll let your dad answer.'

'Like you did your mum, you mean? I couldn't be that much of a shit.'

Nine

The next morning I woke up early for a Sunday, and lay in bed mulling happily over everything that had happened at the party. Then I turned my thoughts to that day, and I squirmed. I hated the whole idea of skulking up to Art's room; I was feeling more and more pathetic about avoiding Fran and Ian. If Art and I hid the fact that we'd got back together, it was like we were ashamed of it. And I wasn't. Far from it.

I couldn't put it off any longer. I had to get out of bed there and then and go round there and – face them. After all, Art had faced Mum. He just hadn't expected to.

I knocked at Art's huge front door half-an-hour earlier than I said I would. I felt it would be better to see them without him around. Fran opened it. She nearly jumped out of her silk kimono when she saw me.

'Col-*ette* ...' she squealed. 'What a surprise!'

'Hello, Fran,' I said. 'Is it really a surprise? Art and I have been seeing each other again. Didn't you know?'

'Darling – no. I had no idea. Look – come in.'

I followed her into her massive, designer kitchen and she said, 'D'you want some coffee? I've just made some.'

'Er ... OK. Thank you.'

'I think Art's still asleep. Unless he didn't come back last night.' And she gave a little mirthless laugh.

She poured out the coffee and motioned to me to sit down. 'Is Ian here?' I asked.

'No. Out running.'

I sighed with huge relief, and said, 'Oh, God, this is seriously embarrassing. I mean – the last time we were in the same room, my mum was screaming at you ... '

Fran reached over and squeezed my hand. 'It isn't embarrassing, Colette. It's lovely to see you again. I was so sorry when you and Art ... broke up. And I admired your mother for what she did. She was protecting you – like a – like a lioness.'

'Rhinoceros, more like.'

'Colette, darling, really! I've been wanting to tell you how sorry I was – that business with the bedroom. I was so wrapped up in my own life, I just didn't ...' She trailed off. I noticed her eyes looked red round the rims. In fact she wasn't her usual polished self at all. 'Anyway!' she carried on brightly. 'What's all this about being back together again, now?'

Just as I was drawing breath to explain, the door opened behind us, and Ian appeared, red and panting and pleased with himself. He saw me and did a double take. 'Good God. What on earth are you doing here?' he said.

'Hello, Mr Johnson,' I answered.

He walked over to the sink and started slooshing cold water on his face. Then he grabbed a towel and turned to face me. 'Have you come to visit Art, or file a complaint against him?' he said.

'*Ian!!*' Fran spat.

I stood up. 'I've come to see him. We've been seeing each other again.'

'You have? Extraordinary.'

'Mr Johnson. Art and I might come from very different backgrounds, and have very different views on things, and ways of behaving, but we ... we like each other a lot.'

He bared his teeth at me. 'Where is Art? Still in bed?'

'I think so,' said Fran.

'I'll take him up some coffee, shall I?' I said, bravely.

There was a potentially explosive pause as Fran hastily poured out another cup. Then she refilled mine, and said, quietly, 'It's lovely to see you again, Colette. It really is.'

And I escaped.

Upstairs, I kicked Art's door lightly, got no answer, pushed it open with one hip and walked in.

He was still in bed. I could see a wad of hair sticking up above the mounds of duvet. I put the coffee down, sat down on his bed, and pulled on the hair, gently.

A lot of groaning and mumbling followed, then his face appeared and his eyes slowly focused on mine.

'JE-sus!' he said, and sat up. 'What *time* is it? I didn't plan this, Coll. I was going to be there to let you in ... '

'Relax. I came early. I decided I had to face your folks. Here's some coffee.'

He took it and drank, eyes fixed on my face. 'You mean you've *seen* them?'

'Yes.'

59

'What happened?'

'Fran was sweet. Your dad was a real sod. But I don't care. I've done it.'

'You're a bit of a hero, aren't you?'

'I'm superwoman. God, I feel good. Last night I got you speaking to Joe again, and today I Faced Your Dad. I'm brilliant. I'm ... '

'Shut up and get into bed with me.'

'No *way*. You smell like a brewery.'

He took another mouthful of coffee. 'I wish I could have seen the old man's face.'

'He wasn't pleased to see me. Not at all. Fran seemed to be, though.'

'She likes you. God knows why.'

'She said Mum was a lioness,' I said, and started laughing. 'And she snapped at your dad. I've never seen her do that before.'

'They've been having a rough time,' Art said. 'Loads of arguments. I don't think they'll last much longer.'

Then he swallowed the rest of his coffee, wrapped the duvet round him and shuffled out of the room. Five minutes later, he reappeared, wet-haired and gorgeous in a huge yellow towel.

'I've had a shower,' he announced.

'Good for you,' I said.

'Coll – '

'No way. Not here. Not now. Not with them underneath.' Then I stood up and wrapped my arms round his damp neck.

'When then?' he said after a while. 'Where?'

'When where what?'

'You know. You know what I mean.'

60

'Here we go again. You're going to have to get over this inhibition you've got about talking about sex, Art.'

'Sod off.'

'You could make use of a dictionary, too. Your vocabulary is really severely limited.'

'Coll,' he groaned, 'if we don't do it soon I'm ... '

'Do it? Do *it*?? You see?'

'Here's fine.'

'No way.'

'They won't care. We could lock the door.'

'*No* way.'

'Last night was so – '

'I know. I know it was. For me too.'

'All right then. We'll go round the back of a bus shelter.'

'You,' I said, 'are absolutely loathsome. Something will turn up.'

Ten

Talking about sex didn't come easily, with Art. Joking, yes, but not talking.

We seemed to talk about everything but ourselves, our relationship together. I was as much to blame as him. I'd have died before I told him how crazy I was about him. It would have been giving too much away.

These stories and adverts where they're so in love and so open — all slow motion running together and frank, open-eyed exchanges of adoration. How can they *do* that? Aren't they *scared*? Scared of what they've got into, scared of what they *feel*? I couldn't look into Art's eyes for long. It was terrifying. It was like a fear of drowning. It was a fear of him seeing too much — a fear of me seeing too much.

Sometimes he'd get into this kind of grim mood, aggressive and silent by turns. Real psycho stuff. I'd get really pissed off with him, and I wouldn't want to be around him. But the energy was still there between us, even so, and we'd always end up kissing again. It seemed to solve everything.

I was caught up in a momentum; I knew sex was the next stage. That was the connection I wanted with him now. Every time we were together, I was bowled over by the way my body seemed to take over, to want more and more from him. I was tired of dreaming, fantasising – I wanted real experience. So those doubts I had, that scary feeling that maybe I was getting in too deep, or that someone like him would get bored eventually and move on – I set them aside. I'd had enough worrying and agonising. Supposing it does go wrong, I said to myself, supposing I sleep with him and then a few months later we split up – it won't be the end of the world. I'll have had that experience. I'll *know*.

I was still worried about actually going through with it, though. 'Going all the way.' It felt like such a long way. You can find out everything in theory but the physical act is still very – well, physical. I tried to talk to Art about it but he just said it would be fine, as though all his experience was some kind of guarantee against anything going wrong.

But I was anxious, underneath. I thought I might seize up or pass out or get hysterical or something. I was afraid it would be a disaster – and underneath, most of all, I was afraid of not measuring up to all the other girls he'd slept with.

I didn't talk about that with him.

We were both tense, waiting. It felt like we were waiting for ever. Nothing else was really important, beside it.

And then we had this opportunity just landed on us about four weeks after we'd got back together. Dad was abroad, and Mum announced she was taking my little sister Sarah out for the whole of Saturday afternoon. I would have the house to myself until the evening.

I told Art. We both knew we'd make love then – we didn't need to discuss it.

Once Mum and Sarah had gone that Saturday, I paced round the house in a state of nerves. It felt so weird, waiting like that, and I felt anything but turned on. It was more like waiting for an exam. Art arrived at about two. I let him in, and he took one look at my frozen face and said, 'Look – we don't have to do this, you know.'

I told him not to be daft, and kissed him, and turned round and went up into my attic bedroom in silence, and he followed.

I stood by the bed, tense as anything, and he stood under the skylight and looked at me. 'I don't want it to be like this,' he said. 'You're different. Go on Coll – use some words.'

But I didn't want to use words. I wasn't there to talk. I went over to him and put my arms round him and said, 'I can't help being nervous. It's one of the few things you know more about than me.'

That made him laugh, and it broke the coldness, the frigidity between us. He got hold of me, and kissed me, and then he pulled off my sweatshirt, and I started to undo his shirt.

'Hey,' he suddenly said. 'The ladder. Your mum thinks if it's down, we can't do it, remember? Suppose she's right?'

It had been one of Mum's house rules that we always left the ladder down when we were up there together.

Giggling, we pulled it up and laid it on the floor. We were shut in together. Then we fell on the bed, kissing and stroking each other, and slowly, we finished undressing each other.

It felt strange and fabulous and scary to be naked with him at last, to feel his chest, his legs against mine. He was kissing me, fast, hungrily, on my shoulders and my breasts, and his hands were sliding all over me, as if he wanted to touch every inch of me. I knew there was no holding back, no going back now. I began to feel I wanted to hide, somehow, I was too exposed, and I was trembling with nervousness. I pulled the duvet all the way over us, and he laughed.

'You can't be cold,' he said.

I couldn't answer. I got hold of him by the hair, trying to make myself brave, and pulled him down to me, and kissed him. He stroked me, caressed me, his fingers clever, slow, but when I slid my hand down his stomach he caught it and put it to his mouth and bit it, gently. 'Don't,' he said. 'I won't last.' Soon afterwards he turned away, and reached over the side of the bed to his jeans. I lay there as he found the condom and put it on. I was waiting, solemn, suspended somehow. He turned towards me, and we held each other, and kissed again, but it wasn't like our other kisses. This is it, I thought, in some fear. I'm crossing into the other country at last. Then he moved between my legs, and began slowly pushing inside me, and I had no more thoughts. The strangeness, the physicality, over-whelmed me.

He barely moved at first, just nudging a little further, a little deeper, while he buried his hands in my hair and our breathing sounded loud, so loud. I was afraid to move. It hurt, as though I was being stretched too far, but I knew I was all right, and I began to know it would all be all right.

It was a long time before he was really inside me. I shut my eyes against the intensity of it, the strangeness – I needed darkness. I wrapped my arms round him, holding on to him – I was so aware of his face against mine, much more aware of his body than my own. He started to breathe faster, move faster, and stronger, until finally he gave an incredible shuddering sigh and slowly folded down on top of me, wrapping his arms round my neck. And I felt a great rush of thankfulness, and even pride, that it had happened so well, and I held his head very close to mine, and started crying.

'Coll – what is it?' He pulled back and looked at me. 'What's wrong? I hurt you!'

I shook my head, still crying.

'I've never been with anyone who's cried before.' He looked as young, as new, as I felt. 'Was it that awful?'

'No. It was ... fine.'

'But why are you crying? Coll – why? Hey – it's over!'

'It's not ... it's not over ... it's begun ...'

Eleven

We lay on the bed holding each other as our breathing got back to normal. I pushed my nose into his hair, where it lay on his neck, and breathed in the soft, brackish smell, and kissed his damp skin. I felt kind of drowned in amazement, and relief, and happiness, that I'd done it, I'd made love with him at last.

Everything was very quiet. The sun had moved beyond the skylight and the attic was darker now, with shadows in the corner of the room. Art was lying completely still, just holding onto me.

Finally, he sighed, and very slowly, he pulled himself away from my arms and started fumbling with the condom. He tied a knot in it and then tossed it onto the floor.

'You OK?' he said, as he turned back to me.

I nodded.

'Coll,' he went on. 'That was ... that was amazing.'

I nodded again.

'I mean – your first time – it's never brilliant ... but that was ... '

'Brilliant,' I said, and I looked at him, willing him to say more. Instead, he got hold of me again, wound his arms round me, lay against me so that every inch of my body was in contact with him.

Maybe words aren't right now, I thought. It was as if our bodies had shared something that our minds couldn't handle, couldn't catch up with yet. It was so precious to me, lying there like that, wound round him. My lover, I said inside my head. My lover.

'Let's go down and get a drink,' he said.

Slowly, as though I was climbing out of a shipwreck, I got off the bed and struggled into my clothes in the half-light, watching Art as he pulled on his jeans. We went down to the kitchen, and I put the kettle on, and Art sat down at the kitchen table with the biscuit tin.

I looked at him as he sat there, chin propped on his hands, chewing. That old table was used for everything – eating and talking, working and arguing. It still had paint splashes on the legs from when first me and then Sarah used to daub on big sheets of paper. I could almost see myself there as a little girl, swathed in a plastic apron, head down, painting away. And now my lover was sitting at the same table. He was smiling his smile, but it wasn't challenging or demanding, like it sometimes was. It was a good smile, a full-up smile.

'What time's your mum supposed to be getting back?' he asked.

'Oh – not yet. They were going to have tea out, she

said. Not till about seven or so.'

There was another silence as I carried the coffee over to the table.

'And your dad's away?' he asked.

'Yes. Until Tuesday. Why?'

'Oh – I'd just hate to be walked in on right now.'

'So put your shirt on. They wouldn't know.'

He smiled at me. 'I feel as though they would.'

I knew what he meant. I felt as though anyone, anyone at all, walking in on us now would know we'd been making love. I felt so different.

As we drank our coffee he reached across the table and got hold of my arm, stroking it. pulling on my fingers. 'You OK?' he said again, and I nodded. I didn't know what to say, what to talk about. I began to find it hard to meet his eye. We finished drinking in silence and then I walked over to dump the mugs in the sink. He came up behind me and put his arms round me.

'It's only five o'clock,' he said into my neck. 'Why don't we go upstairs again?'

I twisted round to face him and we started kissing. The little distance that had opened up between us disappeared. This is our closeness now, I thought, and I was too excited to feel sad about it. This is where we're most together.

I put my hands on his hips and pulled him towards me. I was surprised by how turned on I felt. Wasn't sex supposed to satisfy you? Weren't you supposed to space it out a bit?

'You want to bother to go upstairs?' he said, as we paused for breath and he started unbuttoning my jeans.

'There is *no way* I am doing it in the kitchen,' I said.

69

'How could I help Mum peel potatoes with a straight face again ... '

'Well – come on then,' he said. 'Move it.' So we went upstairs again, and climbed up the ladder.

I pulled it up after me, into the hatch. 'There's no one down there,' he said, laughing.

'I know. I just like the feeling of being cut off up here.'

'With me.'

'With you.'

And I started taking my own clothes off, and he took his off.

'You can do a bit more this time,' he said, when we were lying on the bed.

'No need to make it sound so *practical*,' I answered.

He laughed. 'I'm a practical bloke. Sorry. You're a romantic.'

'Jesus, I'm *not*!' I was quite insulted, for a minute. 'Romantics wear lace and send each other chocolates in heart-shaped – ' I broke off as his mouth landed on mine.

'Oh, shut up, Coll,' he said into my mouth. 'Save your breath.'

So I did. I put all that I'd learnt from him over the past few weeks into practice, and when he groaned with pleasure I felt proud, and powerful. It still felt very new, and a bit alarming, but it was good. This time making love was easier, and slower. I got lost in the rhythm, I was part of the rhythm, I felt I was climbing, climbing, and I heard myself call 'Art – Art – please – ' and then somehow I stopped climbing, I lost it, and I began to wish it would be over, I really wanted him to come so it could stop.

He did climax, soon after, and I wound my arms round him, wanting him, jealous of him, jealous of wherever it

70

was he went to.

'What I don't understand,' he said as he rolled onto his back, 'is why you waited so long. You're an absolute natural for sex.'

I didn't like him saying that. It wasn't sex I was a natural for, it was him. But I just said, 'Well, I had to wait until the right bloke came along, didn't I?'

He turned back and looked at me. 'Well, I'm here.'

I smiled and said, 'Yes.'

Soon afterwards we started to get dressed again, and Art suggested going out, to a pub or something.

'I do not want to be here when the Gorgon returns,' he said, and we both had a fit of panicky giggles.

'Suppose your creepy little sister asks us what we've been doing, or something?' he went on. 'Suppose she *smells* it on us?'

Suddenly it seemed imperative to get out of the house before Mum and Sarah returned. We pulled on the last of our clothes in top speed.

'God,' I said squeakily, remembering, 'the condoms! Where are they?'

'Taken care of,' he said. 'They'll be slapping some surfer in the face off the Cornwall coast soon.'

'Oh *charming*.' I lowered the ladder and we stumbled downstairs. But I was glad I didn't have to dispose of them. Well, to be honest, I was quite glad I didn't even have to touch them. Yet.

We got into town just as the night-life was starting. It felt amazing, strange, walking along beside him, holding hands like we always did, but now everything was different, because we were lovers. Without really discussing it, we went to a pub we rarely go to, because we didn't want to see anyone we knew, not now.

'So would you really have had it off in the kitchen?' I asked him, when we'd got our drinks and were sitting down at a table in the corner.

He shrugged. 'Why not?'

'But *why*? When we had a bed upstairs?'

'Kitchens are OK. I made it in our kitchen once, up against Fran's flashy new cupboards.' He laughed. 'And just before Christmas, they made me go along to this really snobby house with them for lunch, and this girl there, the daughter, laid me in the bathroom. Bathrooms are OK too.'

I stared at him. I felt cold. I felt about 100 miles away from him.

'And I did it at the back of the school hall once – that was really freaky,' he went on. 'We finished just as the caretaker walked in.'

'Jesus, Art,' I said, finally. 'You sound like some kind of pervert.' Although really he'd sounded more like a little boy, boasting. 'What do you need all that high-risk stuff for? Isn't sex itself enough?'

He stared at me. 'Hey – come on. It was only fun.'

'I just – I just don't like hearing about all the other females you've made it with. Well, maybe I do. But not when we've just … we've just … '

He leaned over the table towards me and got hold of both my hands. 'But they were – they were different. You're the first girl I've really liked that I've been to bed with.'

'Been to *bed* with? I thought it was anywhere *but* bed?'

'Come on,' he said. 'It doesn't matter where it is. As long as it's with you.'

72

I felt heaps better when he said that, but I still couldn't get over quite how crass he'd been, listing his Three Daring Places for a Shag only a few hours after we'd made love for the first time. Some instinct kept me quiet, though. If I'd got upset, or indignant, hurt, that would be the last I'd hear about his past, about that side of him. And I didn't want to teach him to cover up, to hide things and feelings because he knew I wouldn't like them. I wanted to know what was inside him, I wanted to know about all of him.

Whatever it was like.

When Art had gone home, I went upstairs and lay on my bed. And everything came back to me, overpoweringly strong. The room seemed to have changed because of what had happened in it.

Twelve

'It was brilliant, Val. And I don't regret anything.'

Val had her self-righteous face on again, the one that made you want to put a fist in it. All-knowing, disapproving.

'It would have been phoney to wait any longer. It really would,' I went on. 'And anyway, I'd made up my mind that even if he told me to get lost right afterwards, I was going to sleep with him. Because I wanted to so much. And once I'd made the decision I felt – I don't know, free. Incredibly powerful, somehow.'

'Incredibly horny more like,' she said.

'Well – that too. But I'd made the decision for me – separate from him. He didn't push me into it.'

'Hah!'

'He *didn't*.'

'Well – I just hope he *has* changed. For your sake.'

'Val — you're not listening to me! It was separate from him, from whether he's changed or not.'

'You really do come out with the most incredible crap sometimes, Coll. How can sex be separate from him? And if it was as brilliant as you say it was, you're going to be wiped out if he suddenly clears off.'

I subsided further into my floor cushion and was silent. It was after school on Monday and we were up in my attic. Val kept giving disapproving glances towards the bed.

'Have you seen him?' she asked. 'Since?'

'No. He had some school thing on yesterday. Don't fold your arms like that — I spoke to him on the phone. Christ, Val, you're out of some handbook from the 1930s called "Making Men Wait Until You're Married".'

'That,' she retorted, 'is not *fair*. It's just — he behaved like such a shit to you. You're worth so much *more*.'

'Look,' I said. 'You're deeply happy and secure with Greg. That's great. But not every relationship has to follow the same pattern. I *know* how it looks from the outside, and I *know* what you think — what everyone thinks — about us getting back together again. But I also know what I feel about Art. And I — I think he feels a lot for me.'

'You think.'

'OK, OK, I know.'

'How do you know? What's he said?'

'Oh, Val, why does it all have to be in *words*?'

'You mean he hasn't told you what he feels about you.'

'Well yes, a bit. I mean not great declarations of love or anything. But it's just so good, when we're together. I've never felt anything like this before. Next to him, every other bloke is just ... nothing. I'm not giving up on it. Anyway, I'd sooner get hurt by someone I feel strongly for, than ... than *not* hurt by someone who does nothing for me.'

'Masochist.'

'Oh, *Jesus*, Val, why don't you *listen* to me instead of ...'

'All right. All *right*! I believe you. You know what you're doing.'

'Col-ETTE!!' It was Mum, bellowing up the stairs. 'It's ART!' The name sang with disgust in her mouth. 'On the PHONE!'

I shot a triumphant look at Val, and ran down the steps to Mum and Dad's room, where the phone extension was. I retrieved it from under Mum's dressing gown and picked up the receiver.

'Hi,' I said. 'Mum? I've got it.' I heard Mum practically smash her end down, and we were alone.

'Hi,' said Art. 'I've got some good news. They're out on Saturday. You can come round.'

'Er – right.'

'After lunch. We'll have the whole house to ourselves.'

'Um – OK.' I suddenly felt really embarrassed, perched there on Mum and Dad's faded duvet cover.

'What's the matter?'

'Nothing.'

'So – are you OK?'

'I'm fine. Well – I've got Val here at the moment, telling me what a big mistake I've made.'

'You've told *her*?'

'Well – yes. You don't mind, do you? We tell each other ... most things.'

'Oh.'

76

'Art – I can't really talk now.'

'Oh. OK. But you can come on Saturday?'

'I think so. Are you swimming on Thursday?'

'Yes. I'll see you then.'

I trudged up to my room again, wondering why I didn't feel more enthusiastic about Saturday. I think it was because the 'first time' had been such a big deal I hadn't really thought about the second time. Not yet. But it was obvious that Saturday was going to be the second time.

'Val,' I said, as I emerged through the loft hatch, 'do you think you'll sleep with Greg?'

She looked at me. 'How do you know I haven't?' she said.

Thirteen

When I met Art at the pool on Thursday, we were different with each other. It was weird, I felt a bit embarrassed, like I didn't know how to behave with him now. He, in contrast, seemed more relaxed than before, more at ease with himself, and with me. He kept grinning at me, which made me more embarrassed.

I suppose he knew where he was now. Maybe for him, our relationship had entered normality.

We stood at the edge of the pool together, just touching.

'What the hell are we going swimming for?' he said, which was more or less what I was thinking.

'Because it's the one time during the week you can get out of the house without being shouted at about A levels,' I said.

We dived in, and swam for a while, then we got

changed and went to the pool café. I watched him as he stood at the counter, getting the coffee, almost as though he were a stranger, and I thought how gorgeous he was. I remembered the first time we'd had coffee together here, after weeks of me idolising him from a distance.

Things haven't changed, I thought. I'm still in a state of obsession. It made my head reel, to think we were together now. It was scary, to have that much.

Art came back with the coffee and sat down. Then he got hold of my hand, and started circling his thumb into my palm, stroking the back with his fingers. 'So you can come over?' he said. 'On Saturday?'

I was enjoying what he was doing so much I didn't answer right away. 'Do you swear your dad won't be there?'

'I swear.'

'I'd die if he opened the door to me. Now that — you know.'

'Don't knock then. Throw stones up at my window.'

'Will you look out for me?'

'Coll. I promise you they won't *be* there! Yes, I'll look out for you.'

It was weird, getting my bike out on Saturday to go round to Art's. I imagined Mum asking me where I was off to, and me brightly replying, 'Oh, just off to have sex, Mum.'

But she didn't see me leave.

When I arrived at Art's house, he opened the door to me. 'Have they gone?' I hissed.

'Coll, for Christ's sake relax. They're not here.'

I followed him into the hall. 'Are you sure?' I nagged.

'*DAD*??' he yelled, really loud, making me jump in fright. 'Fran, you *ZOMBIE*? No – not here.'

When his shout had stopped echoing and my heart had stopped thumping, I felt furious. 'You're really getting off on this, aren't you? You actually wish your old man was here, don't you? Hi, Dad. Coll and I are just going upstairs. Oh – well done, Son.'

'Oh, don't make me puke. If you think there's any of that scoring shit about this, you're wrong, you're really wrong.'

'So why are you looking so smug?'

He laughed. At least he was honest enough not to deny that he was looking smug.

'Because ... OK. Dad's really pissed off about us getting back together. After your mum blowing him out and everything. And I like rubbing his nose in it.'

'Oh, right! So I'm your rebellion, is that it? Your rebellion against your dad? Great.'

'If that's how you want to see it,' he groaned. 'But it's not just ...'

'Well, that's just great,' I ranted. 'That's terrific. It's great to be something you rub your dad's nose in.'

He got hold of me. 'Coll, will you shut up. Forget about *him*! We're doing what's right for us. Well, we would be, if you'd stop grousing and come upstairs.'

I eyed him rather coldly. I wasn't sure how I felt about the speed this was going at. 'You have got a lock on your bedroom door, haven't you?' I said.

He nodded, smiling.

I felt really weird as I walked up the stairs, even more weird than last Saturday. I was in a state of nerves, which is why I suppose I'd been jabbering like that. I couldn't look at Art. It didn't seem to matter, though. It would almost have seemed phoney to talk. The minute we'd got into the room and locked the door, he put his arms round me. Once we were kissing, all the embarrassment just went, and soon we were half-undressed, making love, half on, half off the bed. It was over very quickly. I wanted to carry on moving, moving against him, but I lay still with my arms round him.

Art finished taking off my shirt and started stroking me and kissing me all over. 'Afterplay,' he said. 'I like it better than foreplay.' He moved lower, across my stomach. 'Maybe you'll come now.'

I pulled away and sat up cross-legged on the bed, with the duvet over me. I wondered how Art knew I hadn't 'come'. I wondered if he thought I had at other times, when we'd just been petting. I wondered how he knew.

The thing is, I'm pretty sure I've never had an orgasm, not a real one. I don't masturbate, for a start. I've tried, but I've never got much out of it. And nowadays, with all the stuff about how normal and healthy it is, you feel a bit of an oddball, not going in for what used to be called self-abuse.

And the casual way Art talked about it – it really floored me. He sounded almost practical. What was I, an engine to be revved up?

Suddenly, I just wanted to get my clothes on again. I wanted to be the old me again. I started pulling on my jeans.

'What are you *doing*?' he said. 'We've got hours yet. We've only just started.'

Oh, no, we haven't, I thought. 'Art, I'm really sorry – but I feel weird being here. I want to go.'

81

There was a long silence, then he started to pull on his jeans.

'It's just – look, I'll get used to it,' I said. 'But right now, it's ... too soon after everything that happened.'

'OK,' he said, with as much grace as he could muster.

Then he said, 'You really care what other people think, don't you? I don't feel any different.'

Oh, terrific, I thought. 'Let's go,' I said.

We were both very subdued as we walked into town. We ended up going to see a film, which seemed like a really dreary thing for two people to do when they'd just embarked on an affair together. I felt kind of depressed, let down, as though a different kind of gap had opened up between us.

That Sunday I went round to Val's house and finally got it out of her that she'd started sleeping with Greg, three weeks ago.

'Why didn't you *tell* me?' I wailed. 'I thought we told each other everything ... '

She looked down. 'I don't know, Coll. I just – it didn't seem the right time. With everything that was going on about Art.'

I felt guilt stricken. 'You mean I wouldn't let you get a word in edgeways.'

She smiled. 'Maybe. Also – I don't know. It felt so private.'

There was a chokey feeling in my throat. What she meant was – she hadn't needed to tell me. She had Greg to talk to.

'And the sex is – it's part of everything we have together,' she went on. 'It's not everything.'

She doesn't want to discuss it, I thought. There was this space, this tension, between us. I wandered across her room, and fiddled with the bottles on her dressing table, then I said, 'Val – at the start – did it feel like a major big deal?'

'Well – yes. It still is. But it takes a while for it to get good and ... '

'I mean – the – the *weirdness*. The fact that you're doing that with your body.'

Val looked at me, and said, 'Coll – what exactly is Art getting up to?'

We both had a fit of the giggles. 'It's me,' I said. 'I look at him and it's just ... it's embarrassing. I mean – it's great, too. But I thought it would bring us closer and it hasn't – I mean, I can't see it ever ... becoming normal. Fitting into things.'

Val went off into another paroxysm of laughter.

'Val, shut up. I mean – it's like you can't be relaxed together, like the point of being together now is for sex ... like when you're talking about the weather or something, sex is still there ... and I feel awkward with him. I want to be normal again and just talk, but I can't. It's awful.'

'No, it's not. It's natural. I did with Greg, too. But Greg hadn't slept with anyone before either – we're kind of learning together. And we're good friends.'

'And you're saying Art and I aren't?'

She didn't answer.

Fourteen

Working for A levels was beginning to swallow Art up. He'd had offers from two colleges and he wasn't at all confident about getting the grades; he was really behind on all his revision. He stayed in all week, not even getting out to swim on Thursday. I felt kind of glad for the break. I felt I needed time to adjust to what had happened, to work through it on my own.

On Saturday morning we went out on our bikes. The wind was blowing, buffeting us as we raced along beside each other, first Art in front, then me. We got lost and found our way again; we went for miles, along the river and through the woods. And just when we thought we might die from hunger we found a little pub still serving lunch and ordered homemade steak and kidney pie. Art said he'd pay because he'd just got his allowance. The food steamed and smelt delicious and we ate it ravenously.

'Coll,' Art said, when we were wiping our plates clean with lumps of oaty bread, 'have you ever been on a bike holiday?'

'No – have you?'

'Once. Last year – with Joe. Before that stupid bust-up we had.'

'You mean before you totally betrayed his trust in you as a close friend?'

'Yeah. That.'

'Has he phoned you yet?'

'No. He will. He must be working his arse off too.'

'So – what was the holiday like?'

'Fantastic. We went over to France with Dad and then just took off on our own for a week. Total freedom. You've got everything you need with you – and you just survive.'

'Where did you sleep?'

'Hostels, little places – in the fields. We ought to do it.'

'After your exams?'

'Are you serious? You'd really come?'

'Sure I'd come. What's the matter, don't you think I'm up to it? You're looking at an Outward Bound Supremo here. Totally capable.'

'I know you're capable, Coll. God, that would be great. Would your mum – '

'Once I've got these end-of-term exams out of the way, I'd like to see Mum try and stop me doing *anything* I want to. Anything at all.'

He smiled at me, a real knee-trembling smile, and I smiled back. I was so pleased he'd asked me I'd gone all hot. 'Can you change an inner tube?' he asked.

'No. But you can, so that doesn't matter, does it?'

We set off home, and after a few miles stopped for a breather. I watched Art tip his head back to drink from the water bottle, and I suddenly felt this rush of desire for him, and I realised I hadn't really felt like that since we'd started sleeping together. It was great, it was like coming alive again. I took the water bottle from him and reached up and kissed his mouth, all cold and wet from the water.

'Hrrmph,' he gurgled, swallowing. 'Nice.'

I pressed close, feeling his body all along the length of mine. My lover, I thought. Nothing to fear any more. No more hiding, holding back.

Then he kissed me, and we wound ourselves together by the side of the road. 'Let's go into the woods,' he said.

Without a word, I picked up my bike and followed him into the trees. We found some bracken and lay down on it and kissed some more; then we got half-undressed. It was all very functional, and I didn't care. I didn't *feel* functional.

'Do you always bring Durex along on bike rides?' I whispered.

'Always,' he said.

'Suppose someone comes?' I said.

'That's the idea.'

'Oh, ha ha. Hurry up.'

'What an ... appalling ... thing to say.'

'You ... nature woman,' he said afterwards, looking down at me. 'You're great.'

'Mmmmm.'

'Coll, I know you hate my house. But – they really will leave us alone. We can't always run off to the fields.'

'Why not? D'you get hay fever?'

'I get cold.'

I laughed. 'It'll work out,' I said.

Fifteen

Val had made a decision. She was seventeen in two weeks' time, and because her eighteenth was going to be right before A levels next year, she was going to celebrate being seventeen instead. Her mum and aunt were paying for her to take some friends out to eat at an Italian place nearby, where they let you bring your own wine.

'I went there with Greg, last month,' she said. 'It was really relaxed, really good fun.'

While she was speaking I was planning how I'd sneak round there and ask if I could hide a surprise cake in the kitchen. I'd make something completely gross, covered in jelly beans and Smarties, right up Val's street.

'There'll be about eight of us,' she went on. 'Me and Greg and you, then Caro, Rachel and Dave – not sure about Richard – and Chloe. They've *all* been saying how they never *see* you any more,' she added pointedly.

I waited, hopefully.

'How many's that?' she asked.

'Only eight. Seven – if you don't ask Richard. Which I wouldn't. He can be weird sometimes.' And I waited hopefully again.

'H'm. I don't want to upset him, though. I think I'll ... ' Then she started giggling. 'Your *face*!' she said. 'All right – you can bring Hunk Features along. If you really have to. And he brings champagne.'

I flew forward and hugged her. 'Val, thank you. I really want everyone to meet him – I mean properly. I mean – what's past is past. And he'll be so pleased!'

But when I phoned him, he wasn't a bit pleased. 'Oh, God. Val's that redheaded one, isn't she? She hates me.'

'Well – she has reservations. But this is your chance to win her over. I mean – it'd be nice if my best friend and you could at least *pretend* to get on ... '

'And it's at a restaurant? We have to sit at a table all night?'

'Well, yes,' I said sarcastically. 'You could take yours onto the mat but ... '

'Just don't expect me to make conversation, that's all.'

'No one could expect that, Art. Just sit there and look lush.'

'Yeah – well,' he said grumpily. 'I hate dinner parties. You would too, if you lived with Fran.'

Art was really snowed under with work, now. He missed swimming again that week, but we went out on Saturday night, and then, on Sunday morning, after a lot of persuasion, I went round to his house.

I said a very stilted hello to Ian, who was shuffling

Sunday papers about down at one end of the enormous kitchen; and I had a little chat with Fran, who was doing something complicated with a leg of lamb at the other end. Then Art and I shut ourselves in his room and played music and talked together. After a while I relaxed; I really did feel we were cut off up there, that no one would disturb us.

Then we made love, slowly, in Art's bed.

We're getting better at this, I thought. The awful newness of sex has worn off, and it's something I want now, really want. It's something I can take part in. But I still feel I'm climbing, climbing, and then falling back down.

One day I'll get there. One day I'll arrive.

Towards lunchtime, I said I had to go. 'Don't,' said Art 'Stay here.'

'I told Mum I'd be back for lunch. And I'm hungry.'

'You could eat with us.'

'Art – I can't face your dad now. Not when we've been locked away up here half the day. Anyway, I've got all this course work to do this afternoon.'

'Oh, OK. Creep. I suppose I ought to do some work. I think I'll go back to sleep for a bit first, though. You've worn me out.'

'Art – you shit. If you think I'm going to let myself out ...'

'Oh, OK. Hang on.' He pulled on some tracksuit trousers and together we went downstairs. I tried not to actually run for the door. I really didn't want to bump into Ian.

'When will I see you again?' Art said, as we stood in the porch. He put his arms round me and I fixed my eyes on him. I hated leaving. 'Are you going to the pool?'

'Yes — I think so. Then we've got Val's party on Saturday.'

'Oh, great,' he said unenthusiastically.

'And then we've got another Sunday,' I said pointedly, and pulled myself away, and left.

When I got home, Mum was putting the finishing touches to lunch. 'You were out and about early, dear,' she said comfortably. 'Did you have a nice time?'

I mumbled yes. It can feel weird, leading a double life.

Art and I only met once that week, to go swimming. He had this great habit of putting his arms round me and kissing me as soon as we met up. He'd always done it, from our first date. I reckoned it came from all the kissy-kissy stuff his dad and Fran went in for, but I didn't care about its origins, I just liked it. Most blokes are far too inhibited to touch you right away.

Trouble is, now it carried a kind of agenda with it. I mean, there we were, snogging shamelessly in the sports centre carpark within seconds of saying hello, and he was groaning 'It's been five *days*. Five *days*! Come on, let's go back to my house. Jesus, I can't swim like this.'

Then, once we'd got inside, he tried to get in the changing cubicle with me. It was funny, and sort of flattering I suppose, but it was a pain too. As I pushed the door shut on him he told me how inhibited I was.

'Too *right* I'm inhibited,' I hissed. 'Now get *out*.'

Frankly, he could have done with some of my inhibition. I didn't want to have to be the well-behaved one again, the one who always drew back.

I told Art I had to make Val's cake on Friday night, and he could come and help if he wanted, not that I thought he'd be much help. But he said he'd had a better invitation – he was going out for a drink with Joe. He looked so pleased when he told me, I found myself feeling really protective about him, really hoping it would work out.

Mum had been dead co-operative about Val's cake. She'd bought in huge amounts of marge and flour and sugar, and suggested how to make a big corny seventeen shape: three rectangle wodges of cake, two of them plastered together with butter icing to make a seven. I'd got a really visual collection of sweets together, and seventeen purple candles, and I felt quite excited as I got down to making it.

'D'you have everything you need, Colette?' Mum asked.

'Think so,' I said. She wanted to stay and chat, I could tell, but I wanted to be on my own.

'What have you bought Val?'

'Oh, earrings. I'll show you later. Cornelians.'

'That'll look striking with her red hair.'

Come on, Mum, I thought, out with it. Stop making small chat. That's not your style. Big chat is your style.

'So. How are things?' she went on. 'Generally.'

'Fine.'

'Work going OK?'

'Yes. I got loads done this week.'

'It's such an important time for you. How long to your exams?'

I slammed the flour packet back on the table, and said, 'Mum, you know to the *day* how long it is to my exams. What *is* this?'

She looked down. 'It's just – you seem to be seeing an

awful lot of Art nowadays. I just hope – I hope you'll put your work first.'

I started cracking eggs, really whacking them apart.

'I mean – it's not long to go now. Some of those exams count towards your final grades. They'll affect your whole future. I just hope you're – being sensible. Keeping your feet on the ground. All you've got to do is keep plugging away, and then when they're over – well, think of the freedom you'll have. All summer.'

Mum goes all kind of verbally bulgy when she's like this, when she's skirting round a subject. It was like watching the walls of a dam ready to burst with what she really wanted to say: 'COLETTE – STICK TO KISSING!'

But she managed to contain it. Maybe she didn't think the warning was really necessary. I dreaded to think what she'd say if I told her it was already too late.

Sixteen

Val's birthday cake was a great success – really over the top and yuchy looking. On Saturday night, fizzing with excitement, I took it to the restaurant fifteen minutes early.

I'd arranged to meet Art there. He'd got hold of a couple of bottles of champagne – I didn't ask how. I don't think Ian counts the bottles in his enormous wine rack. We went and hid everything in the kitchen, then we sat at the tiny bar and bought drinks.

Art was silent. I tried to tell myself he was just nervous, about seeing Val again, but I knew he wasn't. He had one of his psycho moods on. He was controlling it pretty well, but I knew it was there, simmering.

'How was your night with Joe?' I asked.

'OK. Well – not good. He hasn't forgiven me yet.'

'Oh. Maybe it was awkward, because it was the first time you'd met up since ... '

'Maybe. There's Val.'

Greg, Dave and Val came in, and I slid off my stool and went to give everyone a hug. I knew they were all shooting semi-hostile glances over my shoulder at Art. Joe wasn't the only person not to have forgiven him yet.

Whenever I'm in a potentially awkward situation, I talk too much. Much too much. I think if I leave absolutely no air space for anyone else, there won't be any trouble.

I babbled inanely as Art joined us and we were shown to the table; I chatted insanely as Caro and Rachel and Chloe arrived. Then Art refilled my glass and said, 'Coll, stop using your mouth so much. Get it round this.'

I didn't mind him saying that – we have this sort of rude relationship. But I could sense Val bristling on my behalf. She and Greg don't insult each other.

Val had ordered a big communal meal when she'd booked the table: it was cheaper that way, and more festive. Soon, mounds of sauce-covered pasta started arriving, and we opened the wine, and Caro fired off a volley of party poppers. Then we all relaxed, and got stuck into the food, and had a great time.

Everyone but Art, that is. He ate and he answered questions and looked at whoever was talking, but he was running on automatic. Part of me was disappointed, but part of me was glad he was keeping a low profile, keeping out of trouble. And if he wasn't exactly contributing, he wasn't spoiling anything, either. His psycho-side was under control.

I focused on Val. I wanted it to be a perfect evening for her, with all her best friends there.

And it would have been, if she hadn't blown it.

Sometimes Val gets sentimental when she's a bit drunk; sometimes she gets aggressive. Tonight, she was aggressive. She baited me good-humouredly about my short dress: then she had a go at Greg for working too hard and not having enough time to see her. Then she started asking Art hostile questions about exams and his plans for the future. He was quiet and non-committal, and wouldn't enter into a fight with her, but I was still very relieved when the waiters cleared our plates and started signalling to me from the kitchen door. I thought a diversion was called for.

'Yes!' I signalled back. 'Now!'

And they carried my cake in, candles blazing. Val was ecstatic. 'This was *you* wasn't it, Coll? Oh – it's *terrific!*' She staggered round the table and threw her arms round me, then she blew the candles out in one gusty puff, and the entire restaurant good-humouredly sang along to Happy Birthday. Dave was busily clicking his camera, recording it for posterity. One waiter popped the corks on the champagne, and another handed Val a huge knife.

'Coll, you're fantastic,' she squealed as she cut the cake into generous slabs with one hand and tipped champagne into her mouth with the other. 'This is the best birthday ever. Here – give some to the waiters. No – not that bit – that's mine. It's got most jellybeans.'

Greg stood up. 'A toast to Val,' he said. 'May she succeed in everything she does. Here's to Val in the millennium!'

'Val in the millennium,' we all gurgled, getting the n's and l's muddled.

'The new millennium is going to be the *women's minnellium*,' shrieked Val. 'You guys had better watch out!'

'Better jobs, better A level grades,' I joined in. 'We are taking *over*!' Everyone laughed. They're used to Val and me doing this sometimes.

'*And* we'll solve pollution. You blokes have – ' Val stopped and glared at Art. 'What's the matter with you? Don't you think it would be a better world if women ruled it?'

'No,' said Art, 'I don't.'

'Oh *yeah*? And why's that?'

'Why should an *autocracy* of women be any better than an *autocracy* of men?'

'Because we're not egocentric bloodthirsty wankers, that's why!'

Art turned to Greg. 'Did you know that's how your girlfriend sees you?'

'You more like!' Val spat back. 'Especially the egocentric bit! I'm sick of men having it all their own way.'

'That is the biggest load of shit. Men don't have it all their own way. They're as trapped as women. You must be really stupid if you can't see that.'

'*Jesus*, Art,' I snapped. 'It was only a *joke*.'

'I'm not too stupid to see what a mess men have made of the world up till now,' Val raged. 'I'm not too stupid to see the way blokes like you *still* behave – and get away with it.'

'I don't know what your problem is,' said Art. 'Well, I can take a guess. But I've put up with you snarling at me long enough.' He stood up, and looked down at me. 'You coming?' he said.

Val stood up too. She faced Art, square. 'She doesn't have to do what *you* say,' she spat.

'Maybe she wants to,' he sneered

Then Val smacked him in the face, really hard.

Seventeen

Instinctively, I grabbed Art's right arm. He shook me off. 'I'm not going to hit her,' he snapped. 'I just want to get out of here. Are you coming?'

I was panic-stricken. What the hell had happened? Everyone was sitting there, stunned. I felt for Val, and I felt for Art. And I couldn't take sides. Not between them.

'Oh, *Jesus Christ*!' I erupted. 'You two do my *head* in!' Then I turned and ran out of the restaurant. If I got out, I wouldn't have to choose between them.

I pelted round the block and stopped. I was shaking, a little. What do I do now? I thought. Just go home? Then I heard running footsteps behind me. I turned; it was Greg.

'Hey,' he called. He caught up with me and put his arms round me. 'Hey. You all right?'

'Have you left those two together?' I asked, anxiously. I had visions of them beating each other to death.

'Relax. Art's gone. Val's enjoying the drama.'

'*Enjoying* ...'

'Yes. Face it, Coll, whacking Art like that was a kind of bonus birthday present for her.'

'*What?*' I wailed. 'I thought she'd be really upset. That her party's been spoilt ...'

'It hasn't been spoilt. It was great. It just had a – spiky ending.'

'*Spiky?* She smacks Art in the face and you call it spiky? Why'd she *do* it?'

'Oh, come on. She's wanted to thump him ever since you split up. She thinks you made a mistake, getting back with him. She thinks he's using you.'

'Well, she shouldn't have let him come, then, if she thinks that.'

'She let him come for your sake. She thought it would be OK. But then when he sat there not saying anything – well, she thought he was being superior. A superior git, to be precise. At least that's what she yelled after him as he left.'

'Oh, God. Poor Art. I'll kill her. She behaved like a complete thug.'

Greg started to stroke my hair. 'Coll. Coll. She doesn't trust him. She doesn't want you to get hurt.' Then he added, 'I don't, either.'

I pulled away. 'Why doesn't anyone trust *me*?' I said. 'I know what I'm doing.' I started to walk off.

'Where are you going?' Greg called after me. 'It's nearly midnight, Coll. Don't just go like that.'

'I'm going round to see Art,' I said.

I half-ran, half-walked all the way to Art's house. I felt I had to see him, I had to fix things. When I got there I knocked on his door, loudly. Ian opened it. I took a huge breath and said, 'I'm really sorry it's so late, but could I see Art please?'

He smiled at me, eyebrows raised, dead superior. 'Colette, have you been knocking my son around?' he said.

Immediately, I went bright red. 'No. No, not me. My — my friend.'

'Some friend,' he murmured, as he turned on his heel. 'He'll have a black eye in the morning. He's through in the kitchen.'

Art was sitting hunched at the table, nursing a mug of tea. He looked at me coldly. I'd obviously interrupted a man-to-man talk. And I could imagine the advice his dad had been giving him.

'Art,' I began, 'I'm sorry ... I'm really sorry. I don't know what got into her.'

Art didn't reply. Ian, behind me, said, 'Well — I'll leave you two to it,' and walked out.

I felt a kind of panic as I stood and looked at Art. I didn't know how to put things right again. I went and sat next to him, and put a hand on his shoulder. 'Let me see your face,' I said. 'Your dad said you'll have a black eye ...'

He shrugged me off. 'I'm OK,' he said.

'Val will be feeling awful now,' I ventured. 'Really sick at herself.'

He didn't answer.

'What happened when you saw Joe?' I asked.

He twisted round and glared at me. 'Joe? What the hell's he got to do with it?'

'Well — you seemed really down, all evening. I wondered what had happened.'

'What the *hell* has that got to do with anything? I was *fine* until your friend smacked me one. God, I wish I'd hit her back. I hate girls like that.'

'She's *not* usually like that. She honestly isn't. I've never seen her hit anyone before — ever.'

'Great. So something about me tipped her over the edge, did it?'

'I don't know. I haven't spoken to her.'

'No, you cleared off pretty quickly, didn't you? And all your friends just stood and stared. It was beautiful.'

I suddenly saw it as it must have been for him, standing there humiliated, surrounded by my hostile friends. I slid my hand round his neck, and bought my face close. I wanted to cry. 'I'm sorry,' I muttered. 'I shouldn't've run out. I just ... I didn't want to take sides.'

'Take *sides*? If one of my friends had hit *you* ... '

'Art, I'm sorry,' I said again.

'I looked for you,' he went on. 'I came back to look for you. Then I saw you with Greg.'

'Oh — Art. I didn't see you. Why didn't you come over?'

'Because he had his arms round you.'

'But that's just — '

He shrugged. 'I went home.'

There was a pause. 'I'll never fit in with your friends,' he went on. 'You and I are so different.'

'Don't say that,' I pleaded. 'We're not. And you don't have to fit in with them.' I wanted him to touch me so badly I couldn't bear it. I wrapped my arms round him, and hugged him, but he didn't respond. 'Art, please,' I

101

said. 'Don't do this to me.'

'Do what?' he said bleakly.

'Look – I'm here. And I've said I'm sorry. It's just well, I didn't think of sticking up for you. You're usually so in control.'

There was another silence. Then I said, 'What did happen? What happened with Joe?'

'Why d'you keep asking that? Nothing happened.'

'It did. I know it did. You were so quiet this evening ...'

He stared straight ahead at the table. Then he said, 'Joe told me he was glad we'd met for a drink, to ... get things straight. We talked for a bit. Then he told me how he'd never trust me again.'

'Oh, but he can't have meant ...'

'That's exactly what he meant.'

'But at Stephanie's party, he seemed so – I thought you'd made up.'

'He said he'd done some thinking since then. He'd decided he couldn't just – bury it all. He said I'd only understand if it happened to me.'

I hugged him tighter. 'Why didn't you *tell* me?'

'Ten minutes before Val's party? Anyway, I was OK.'

'Until you got whacked.'

He smiled. 'Yeah. Till then. Coll –'

'What?'

'When I saw you and Greg together ... I thought it *was* happening to me.'

'Oh, crap. You know we're just friends.'

'But it made me feel – I don't know. What I did to Joe. He said he hasn't had another girlfriend since.'

'Give him time,' I said. 'He needs time to get used to –'

I was interrupted by a timid tap on the door. Fran poked

her head into the room.

'Sorry to interrupt,' she murmured, 'but it's nearly two o'clock. Will your mum be getting worried, Colette?'

'Oh, God. Yes – I ought to go.'

Then Fran said, 'I could phone her, if you like, and put her mind at rest. I'll say Art got very drunk and you saw him home and ... and you're staying over in the spare room. It's only a white lie, really, isn't it?'

I looked at Art. I wanted to stay. I wanted to stay so much. I wanted to get close to him again. He looked back at me, and said, 'Yes. Thanks, Fran.'

Eighteen

I didn't stay in the spare room. We lay side by side in his bed for what seemed like ages, not talking, just holding hands. I longed for him to put his arms round me, but everything that had happened that night was still between us. It chilled me to think how I'd made all these assumptions about Art: that he was somehow unhurtable. He wasn't. Joe had hurt him. And I'd hurt him. I'd hurt him more than Val had.

I turned on my side and started kissing him, kissing his neck and his chest, kissing the bruise starting on his eye. After a while he began stroking my hair, and then I kissed him on the mouth, and soon we were wrapped up in each other, beginning to be healed. I wanted him so much, so much, and everything seemed to fuse, every-thing came together – 'Shhhh,' he said, putting his hand to my mouth. 'Ssshhhhh!'

I buried my face in his shoulder and held him close. I wanted to stay in the blackness for ever.

The next day I woke up before Art, and stared at the light filtering through the blinds. I thought about making love the night before. I must have come, I thought. It wasn't all definite and separate like I'd expected an orgasm to be. It was part of the whole night.

I wrapped my arms round Art's sleeping body. 'Let it be OK,' I prayed. 'Let all the crap that happened last night just … not be here any more.'

But when he woke up he had retreated, a little. I suppose if you're like Art and you show someone you've been hurt you do back off a bit, the next day. We were quiet together. He brought some tea and toast up to the room and soon afterwards I got dressed and went home. I knew I had to go back sometime.

When I let myself in, Mum was in the hall. I felt naked, as though she was peeling layers off me with her eyes. 'So!' she said. 'You knew Art's stepmother phoned me last night, I take it?'

'Yes – sorry, Mum,' I said, trying to remember what excuse Fran had said she'd use. 'Did it wake you? Art was really the worse for wear. Well, so was I. It was a great party.'

'H'm. Well, Val's been on the phone already. She sounded worse for wear, too.'

'Ah, well, it's only once a year!' I said in a phoney, jolly voice, and escaped.

I went into Mum's room and phoned Val. The minute she heard me she kind of overflowed.

'Oh GOD, you're back! Coll, I feel *dreadful*. I am really,

really sorry. I don't know what got into me. God. How's … how's Art?'

'Bruised,' I said, pointedly.

'I was pissed. I was out of control. I just snapped. You'd been so sweet, with the cake and everything, and then I looked at him, and I … it's what I wanted to do ages ago, when you split up with him, and I'd … you know, repressed it, and then it re-emerged … '

'Val. Please. Spare me the psychology. Look – it's OK. I mean – it'll be a while before we all go out in a foursome, but it's OK. Forget it. You don't like him, that's all … '

'Och, it's not that I don't *like* him. I mean – I don't, much, but it's the way he … '

'Val, I'm tired. Really tired. I have to get some sleep. And look – I don't care any more about what you and Greg think of him, OK? I know you mean well, and I don't blame you, but from now on – it's my life, OK?'

'Yes,' she said humbly. 'I'll butt out.'

'What I mean is – ' I said, softening a bit, 'I'm in too deep. It's not like I can make any sort of decision about it … Do you understand?'

'I think so,' she said. 'Coll?'

'What?'

'Oh, Coll. I just can't bear the way he's taken you *over*.'

I was silent, knowing that was the real reason why she'd hit him. 'He hasn't, Val,' I said. 'I know it looks like that but – it's just very weird at the moment and – look, please don't stop being my friend, OK?'

Val laughed. She sounded so pleased and full of relief it

amazed me. 'Don't be an idiot,' she said. 'It would take more than him to stop us being friends. And Coll – ?'

'What?'

'Thank you for my cake. It was great. It really was.'

Nineteen

Art and I met in a pub that Thursday. He seemed a bit distant, still. I told him about phoning Val, and her agreeing to back off, but he didn't do much more than shrug. We chatted half-heartedly for a while, but he wouldn't discuss what had happened with Joe any further. He said it was in the past now. After a while I said, 'Why don't you ever talk about your past? Like – your old girlfriends?'

He stared at me. 'What's there to talk about? Most of them weren't around for very long.'

'And was that their decision or yours? That they weren't around for long?'

'It was mutual, usually. I can't remember. Who cares.'

I sat back, rebuffed. 'I just want to know,' I said. 'I'm interested.'

'Oh, Jesus, Coll. They weren't so hot. Some of them

were good shags, and some of them weren't.'

'Oh, great. You have such a way with words.'

There was a silence.

'Sometimes,' I said, 'I feel like just another one in a line.'

'No, you don't,' he said. 'They were different to you.'

'Why?'

'Jesus, Coll, you know why. With them it was just — with you it's — it's all part of the same thing with you.'

'Is that supposed to make sense?'

'I mean sleeping with you is just ... part of it. Sex was like — separate with them. And it's not with you. If we're getting on well — it's better than if we're not.'

'That's some analysis, Art. Maybe you should take up psychology.'

'Shut up. What I'm trying to say is — it's part of everything we have together. You're special, Coll. You know you are.'

I made some silly reply, and reached for my drink, and we started talking together. But I'd gathered those words into me, gathered them in like precious stones, to save them for later, for when I was alone and could enjoy them properly.

After the night of Val's party, Fran became a real ally. When I went round the following weekend, she seemed really pleased to see me, asking me how I was and getting me a glass of juice. As I was finishing it off she put her hand on my arm and said in a confidential voice, 'You know, darling — he hasn't had any other girls round here. Since you.'

I stared at her. All I could think of to say was 'I should

bloody well hope he *hasn't*!' and that seemed a bit inappropriate, because Fran seemed to think she was letting me into some really special news. So I just said, 'Hasn't he?' in a deadpan voice.

She sighed and said, 'I'm so glad you're back together again. You're so good for him, Colette.'

I told Art what she'd said, about not having other girls round since me, and he laughed. We made love, daylight love, nothing like last Saturday with its blackness and escape. Afterwards I got up and put his shirt on and wandered round the room, looking at books on the shelves and the things on his desk. Then I went back and sat beside him and said, 'So how many women have you had up here, then?'

'*Jesus*, will you stop going *on* about that? Hundreds, I had bloody hundreds – they used to form a queue at the door.'

'Oh, ha, ha. Sleaze.'

'You ought to be grateful you've got such an experienced ... '

'Be *what*?'

'Grateful.'

I shoved him half off the bed. 'No need to be so sour,' he said. 'Just because you didn't come.'

I felt like he'd hit me. At first I thought he was taunting me. But then I made myself look at him and I knew he wasn't.

'What do you mean?' I said, almost in a whisper. Then I said, 'How do you know?'

He laughed. 'How do I *know*? Oh, come on, Coll. When you come, I'll *know*.' He put his arms round me. 'You sort of did last Saturday, didn't you?'

I didn't know what to think. I felt incredibly embarrassed, and somehow moved – that he'd said it, that he'd had the courage to say it. He was supposed to be the one that found openness hard. And I realised he was right, I was feeling frustrated, left out. Sort of angry with him.

'I feel like I'm climbing, heading up to something – and then it just goes away, falls away,' I said, into his shoulder. 'I don't know. It's not supposed to be everything, though, is it?'

'No, no – it's not,' he said carefully. 'But it will happen for you, I know it will.' There was a pause, then he added, 'You're too much of a demanding cow for it not to happen.'

I laughed, reached up and worked my fingers into the hair at the back of his head.

'We just need lots of practice,' he said.

And I heard myself saying, 'OK. So let's practise.'

We took our time. I made him lie still, face down, while I massaged his shoulders and his back. Then he made me lie still. I felt very warm towards him, and open. We were very slow, very sensual, and just when I thought I'd go crazy with everything he was doing, he pushed inside me. This time it lasted, it built, and then it was happening for me, and I knew I didn't have to try for anything, reach out for anything, because it was all there, flooding over me, happening, happening, so much I couldn't hold it.

'Oh, *God*. Oh, God, that was brilliant. Oh, *God*.' I rolled away, and stuck my head under the pillow. I found myself wanting to carry on crooning to myself, so I did, under the pillow.

'Come out, Coll,' Art said, laughing. 'Come *out*.'

Don't spoil it, I thought. Don't say anything.

He pulled the pillow away from me and kissed me, and I felt as though all the other girlfriends he'd had just fell away, back, back into the past, and all that mattered was now.

Afterwards was magic. It was too important to talk about, but it was there between us. We were giggly and stupid and tender together.

I put his shirt back on. 'You look dead sexy in that,' he said. 'Great legs. Let's go and get a drink. I'm de-hy-drated.'

We went and raided the fridge. Art found half a bottle of white wine. I found some prawns. He found some grapes. I found a half-empty box of chocolates. He found some flat fizzy water. It was like a celebration.

'Let's go,' he said. 'We can have a food orgy up there. I'll smear this stuff over you like in that film ... '

'I thought I heard scavengers in here.'

I froze. It was Ian, in the doorway. I'd thought he was out. Actually, I'd forgotten all about him.

'Emptying the fridge, are you?'

'Hi, Dad,' Art said.

'Hello, Colette,' Ian said, drily. 'You're looking relaxed.'

I could feel my face glowing red, redder. Down to my neck, down to the neck of Art's shirt, down to my knees. Down to my bare feet.

'Come on, Coll,' Art muttered, and we shuffled past, clutching our loot, and back upstairs. As he kicked the bedroom door shut, I started to shriek quietly. 'Oh, *God*, how embarrassing! I nearly died down there! "You're looking *relaxed*"! Aaagh!'

'Oh, sod him. Come on – let's eat.'

'But now he *knows*. He *knows*!'

'Coll – I think he knew before.'

'Oh GOD!'

'Relax, Coll. As far as *he's* concerned, we've been really slow getting round to this, right?'

'Oh. Right.'

'He just wanted to make his point. The prat.'

Once we'd locked the door again, and I'd had a swig of wine, my embarrassment abated a bit, and I began to feel fabulous again.

We spread all the food out on the bed. I peeled the prawns, sucked the juice from the heads and then chewed the flesh.

Art looked at me, full of admiration and disgust. 'You animal,' he said. 'How can you *do* that?'

'S'delicious. Try one.'

'No thanks. It looks like a woodlouse. And stop dropping shells on my bed.'

I took another swig from the wine bottle. 'I can't believe I went down there in your *shirt*. Still, I suppose your dad's used to half-dressed girls drifting round the kitchen.'

'Coll. For Christ's sake. I am not proud of all that shit I was into. For the last time, can't you drop it?'

I smiled. 'OK,' I said.

Over the next few weeks, things got into a pattern. I spent long hours in his room every weekend; we'd work together, and talk and make love. Slowly, uninterrupted, very sure of each others' bodies now, very sure of all the different ways you can make love. It was amazing, the freedom we had. We still went swimming, and sometimes we'd take the bikes and head into the country somewhere, and make love there too. Apart from one terrible party, we didn't see any of his friends at all. I suppose we were pretty isolated.

Something had happened to me. Something had got hold of me, something so strong and fierce it was always with me, even in the bad times, even when I was fed up. It was wanting Art, wanting only to be with him. I'd been crazy enough about him at the start but this was different. My self-protectiveness had gone. I was getting deeper and deeper in.

I was too sophisticated to call it falling in love. I hate it, the way people throw that word around: 'But do you love him?' and 'I love him, I really love him' and 'Come on, you know how much I love you.'

It's crass.

I didn't have a word for what I felt.

I saw less of Val, but we met up at school. Things were going well for her and Greg, she said. They had no inhibitions about saying they loved each other. He was always buying her presents – funny little tokens, books inscribed with loving messages, earrings, T-shirts. She'd show me, smiling with pleasure, saying, 'Honestly, he's so soft.' I'd admire the latest offering and try to imagine Art buying me earrings. Or a book. Or anything at all, really, and I couldn't.

She said there's nothing they can't talk about. They're so close, so secure. She says she has two best friends, now.

Part of me envied them. Somehow, I couldn't see Art as a friend. Friends don't hurt you, and I felt he had the

114

power to hurt me more than anyone I'd ever met. I couldn't just relax and be open with him, not about everything. It would have been giving too much away.

And in some ways I liked the distance between us, the difference between us – the energy between us. I didn't want to be all safe and cosy and confidential with him. That wasn't what he was for.

Twenty

Art's A levels were only three weeks away. He was getting increasingly tense about them. And I was dangerously behind on my revision and my course work, too. That Saturday I locked myself up in my attic. I reckoned I had about two weeks to catch up on, and if I worked Saturdays from now on I'd be OK. Just.

I felt exhausted with boredom before I even started. You've got to get a grip on yourself, girl, I said, as I opened my history folder. It crackled, dry, dead, repellent. Get some revision done, I nagged myself. You've got to.

But I couldn't concentrate. I couldn't even sit still. Exams were coming at me like an express train and all I could think about was losing myself in Art's body, in my body ... what was happening to the old me, the old me who used to be able to work? Who was this new Coll, all shag-happy and swoony and mindless?

It's the power of nature, I thought. Nature wants me bonded with a man to carry on the species, and Nature doesn't give a toss about qualifications. Nature is a great baby-factory owner who sees me as one more female on the production line. Get her hooked, then she'll produce half-a-dozen kids and then whap, finished, menopause, out of the exit chute, out on her ear.

Well, not me, I said determinedly, and I drew the grey file towards me again. There is more to life than being with Art, it's just that I seem to have forgotten what it is right now.

I set to work and then after five minutes I was looking moonily up at the skylight, thinking about him touching me, me touching him. I was seriously fed up with myself, I can tell you.

In the end the only way I could get myself to revise was by threats. I told myself that I had to get to the end of my history file, taking notes and listing the gaps I needed to fill in, before I saw Art again. It worked. I actually got down to it. I cancelled my Saturday night out, deaf to all Art's attempts to persuade me not to be so boring and 'just come over for an hour or two'. I got up early Sunday. And by lunchtime, I'd finished. I phoned Art and crowed at him.

'Well done, star,' he said. 'Come round for lunch. They've got a load of people coming. Fran's roasting half a cow. Two o'clock.'

I had half an hour to get ready. I sang in the shower as I washed away all the studious lankness of my hair, all the staleness of sitting hunched over my books. 'I *can* do both,' I sang, 'I *can*. I have *earned* this!' I pulled on a new top I hadn't worn yet. I slapped on some lipstick. I glowed. 'It's with virtue,' I told myself.

Downstairs, I told Mum I'd done nothing but work for the last thirty-six hours and now I'd been asked for lunch with Art but they'd be dishing up in seven minutes and it was raining hard and could she *possibly* ...

Dad got to his feet, laughing. 'Get in the car,' he said. Come on, Justine, she deserves it.'

And in ten minutes I was there.

'So,' I said into Art's mouth as he got hold of me by his front door, 'how much work have *you* done? I can take the rest of the day off.'

'Great. Me too.'

'You mean you've done some revision?'

'Enough. Just because I don't phone people up to *boast* doesn't mean I don't put the hours in.'

Lunch was a riot. There were ten or more people there, and it was noisy, and wine was flowing, and Art and I managed to sit together at one end of the table and ignore everyone. We behaved very badly; we laughed together and talked practically nose to nose and shut the others out. We were hungry and hedonistic. Under the table, Art had his hand on my leg which was pressed hard against his leg. No one took any notice of us. Fran kept filling our plates in an absent sort of way.

As soon as we could, we sloped off upstairs, hand in hand. No one noticed us go; no one would have cared if they had. The minute he'd shut the door we fell on each other, and started necking.

'So, was it worth it?' Art said, when we surfaced for a breath.

'Worth what?'

'Not seeing me all week. Just to work.'

'Yes, it was. Easily.'

118

'You're a swot. A real swot.'

'Yup. I'm going to get all As.'

'I like your top thing.'

'It's new.'

'Take it off.'

Laughing, I pulled away and walked over to the window. Art followed. Beside his desk stood a big, lopsided Swiss cheese plant. One newly opened leaf reached out its fingers to the light.

'Where did this come from?' I said.

'Fran chucked it out. She said it was getting too big and crude, which is exactly what she thinks about me. So I felt this bond with it. I rescued it from the dustbin.'

'But it's still healthy – look at that new leaf. Fancy just chucking it.'

'That,' he said, 'is my stepmother for you. But he's safe now, aren't you, mate?'

Then he went and bolted the door, turned round, and peeled his sweatshirt off.

We made love slowly, like something we'd deserved. It built and built, full of urgency, but sure, nothing rushed. Afterwards we stayed curled up on the bed together and slept. When I woke it had got quite dark. Outside, the street lights were coming on in the lane alongside the house, bringing a weird orange glow into the room. Shadows were moving on the walls; the big new leaf of his plant made a shape like a great hand reaching over us. The rain had got heavier, splashing on the windows and sounding along the gutter outside, gurgling like a stream. I moved closer to Art. Everything was suddenly so significant, the rain, and the shadows, and the unnatural light. It was all so real to me, more than real, overreal, as though

119

my senses were heightened, honed, like a mystic in a trance.

'I am advancing onto the astral plane,' I whispered to Art. 'Without the aid of illegal substances.'

He grunted. He was still half asleep. I studied his face, pushed the hair back from his eyes. That space between his eyebrow and his eyelashes was so lovely, that line between nose and mouth ... and the smooth skin on his chest, over his muscles ... I felt as though adoration was pouring out of me, so strong you could see it, like one of those paintings of Christ, where love is shown as streams of light.

'I'm having an altered state here,' I said, pulling his hair tenderly. 'I'm ... Light is pouring all over you, Art – my light. Wake up, you sad bastard. You'll miss it. I feel – I feel amazing.'

He smiled up at me through half-closed eyes. 'Good. I'm a great shag,' he said, and went back to sleep.

When I got home that evening I sat at my desk under the skylight and pulled a bit of paper in front of me. I wanted to write something that would let me remember how I'd felt in his room. And what I wrote was a sort-of poem. I wrote it straight off, with hardly any changes:

> The glow from outside, orange,
> And dark splashes of shade on the wall,
> Especially the fingered shadow of your plant.
> And the sound of rain
> Ceaseless, comforting
> Binding us closer, here with no clothes on,
> Here on the bed in the almost-warmth.

When I read it over, I thought it said it all — the specialness, and the way I liked how he'd rescued the plant, and the way all my senses had been so alive, and even the little cold bit at the end, the bit that described the distance between us.

I decided I'd give the poem to Art. I couldn't say it to him, but I could write it.

After our swim on Thursday, when we were sitting in the café, I handed him the poem. 'This is for you,' I said.

After he'd read it, he looked up at me. I realised I'd been holding my breath. 'Well?' I said.

He turned the sheet of paper upside down, and looked at it again.

'Oh, ha, ha. Don't you like it?'

'Um. What's it mean?'

'It's describing a moment of presence — you know, last Sunday. When I felt really ... alive. It was brilliant.'

'Coll, if you wanted to write about something brilliant, why didn't you write about us having it off?'

'Because that would be pornography.'

'It's ... great, Coll,' he said. 'Can I keep it?'

Maybe we're spending too much time shut up in his room together. Maybe it isn't healthy. Art can't get over it, the way making love affects me. He feeds on all the changes I go through. He says I enjoy it more than he does. Maybe I do.

He doesn't know what's going on inside me — feelings of worship, gratitude, adoration. I keep that well inside me. I think it would scare him silly if I let it out. But I express it in my own way. I travel every inch of him, and love him, and he doesn't realise it's love, he thinks I'm just

121

very sexy, very adventurous, great in bed. And I let him go on thinking that, I let the doubleness exist, because I can't at the moment see how it could be any other way.

Love. I love him. It doesn't sound crass any more. But I can't tell him. I'm waiting for him to speak first.

I've started to notice the lyrics of all those old songs – about love being dangerous, love is a drug, love chains you up. I know what they mean now.

Twenty-one

Two days later, the pattern was broken.

Suddenly. Brutally.

Saturday morning, just as I was slowly finishing breakfast before getting down to another study session, Val arrived at my door. She was white, distracted. I made her a coffee, and we went up to my room. 'Val,' I said, 'what on earth's wrong?'

She looked at me, her face crumpling, and said, 'I think I'm pregnant.'

It was like all the air had been sucked out of the room. I felt this terrifying pressure. 'Why?' I said, trying to sound calm. 'How late are you?'

'A week.'

'Oh, Val, that's nothing! You're worried — because of the exams and — '

'But you know I'm never more than a day or so late.

123

And – a while back, we … we were careless.'

'Oh, God.'

'He withdrew. He said it was OK. I know we shouldn't have done it. We – we'd run out – we – '

I got hold of her hand. 'Val, don't panic. Have you … ?'

'I feel like I'm going to come on! I feel all – bloated, awful! But nothing happens!'

'Val. There's tests you can do – even if you're only a few days late. Accurate tests.'

She stared at me, wide-eyed.

'From the chemist,' I said. Then I stood up. 'Stay here. I'll go and get you one.'

I grabbed my purse and ran all the way. Then, when I got to the chemist, I walked straight past. I just couldn't go through the door. 'Don't be so *pathetic*,' I said to myself. 'It's not you, it's Val. Go back and *go in*!'

I tried to remember those condom adverts that told you the sales assistant couldn't care less what you were buying. I walked in and hissed to the girl behind the counter, 'Can you recommend a pregnancy testing kit?'

She produced a box and waved it in front of me. I heard the words 'reliable'; 'accurate', 'you can use it the day after a missed period' and I managed to smile and say great, thanks, and hand over the huge amount of money she seemed to be asking for. Then I ran home.

We unwrapped the jolly, pastel-coloured box and took out a stick thing, and I read the instructions. 'Go on, Val,' I said, 'just take it in the loo and pee on it.'

She looked at me, terrified. 'But what if … '

'You've got to *know*,' I barked. 'Go on. Do it. If it's all a false alarm … '

Minutes later she appeared. She showed me the stick.

'One dot shows it's working,' I croaked. 'If a second dot appears after five minutes or so, it means you're pregnant.'

I could see the second dot forming already. Maybe that's just because it's still wet, I thought. Maybe it'll go away after the five minutes you're supposed to wait — maybe it'll fade.

It didn't, though. It stayed. It was like a beacon. I'm here, it said.

I'm here.

Twenty-two

Val broke down and cried when the fact that she was pregnant sunk in. 'Oh, God,' she sobbed. 'What am I going to *do*? Oh, God. I feel sick.'

I held her and stroked her hair, awkwardly, mechanically. My mind was screaming: why did this have to happen, why did this have to happen? I can't help you alone. Oh, Christ. I don't know what to do. I don't know what to do.

And then, through the attic hatch, Mum's head, summoned by the crying. And like in a dream, when you can read other people's minds, I looked at Val, and she buried her head in my side, and I knew that meant 'yes', and I said, 'Mum? Val's ... she's pregnant.'

And like in a nightmare, Mum's face darkened, and she heaved herself up the steps, and walked over to us. And she lifted Val off me, and put her arms round her, and said,

'All right, Val. It's all right.'

We went down to the kitchen and drank tea, and let Val weep, and tried to comfort her. She was still in a state of shock, of disbelief. Dad came in once and after a look from Mum, left immediately.

'You're going to have to accept it, dear,' Mum was saying. 'These tests aren't wrong – this way round. Sometimes they can miss a pregnancy – but they don't indicate one if it's not there.'

'What am I going to do?' wailed Val. 'I can't tell Ma. I can't.'

Val's family were Irish Catholic. Lapsed, yes, but Catholicism was there in their roots and their blood.

'Val, don't panic,' Mum said heavily. 'How late are you?'

'A week,' sobbed Val.

'So you're ... you're only five weeks pregnant.' She reached over and squeezed Val's hand. 'You've got plenty of time to – think things over. If you decide you want an abortion, it's ... well, it's too early to do one, at the moment. The ... the foetus is too small for them to be sure they've carried out the operation successfully.'

Val started crying again.

'Colette – go and phone Greg,' Mum said. 'Tell him to come round. He has to know, Val.'

It was one of the most horrible phone calls I've ever had to make. Greg knew why I'd phoned, of course, almost as soon as he heard my voice, strained and different. Val would have shared all her worries with him, and I think something in him knew the worst already.

He was at our door within fifteen minutes, ashen-faced. He came into the kitchen and put his arms round Val, and she stood up, and together they went to the door.

'We'll go and ... we'll go for a walk or something,' he said. 'Thank you. Thank you, Mrs Rowlands.'

Mum patted his shoulder. 'I'm here,' she said. 'I'm here whenever you want me – either of you. You know that.'

He shot her a look of desperation, and left.

'They're such children,' she said, her eyes filling. 'Such children themselves.'

By the end of the day I felt exhausted by the effort of worrying about Val and trying to work. I didn't phone Art. Somehow, I didn't want to talk about it with him.

I told Mum I'd skip supper. She understood. She made me some toast, and told me to go to bed. I cried into the pillow for a while, and then I tried to reread *Lord of the Flies*, one of our set books, to take my mind off everything. But it seemed so alien, so unimportant, all these little boys with their fear and their cruelty, and I couldn't follow it.

Later, Mum brought me up some tea, and sat down on the bed.

'Colette,' she said, stroking my hair. 'You did the right thing, telling me. And you've stood by Val, and you'll help her. You're a good friend.'

I started crying again, crying like a little girl, and Mum put her arms round me and rocked me to and fro. I felt her strength and her solidness, and I wept.

'What do you think she'll do?' I sobbed. 'What do you think she'll decide?'

'I don't know. It's a terrible decision, either way. Have you ever talked about it?'

'No. Not really. I mean – I think we just thought – we weren't going to let it happen. And if the worst came to the worst – we said we'd have an abortion. But now that

128

seems so ... it seems so ... '

'Yes,' Mum said. 'I know.'

'And it's Greg's decision, too,' I wailed.

'I know, I know. But mostly it's Val's. It has to be.'

'Why did this have to happen *now*? I can't bear it. How can she do her exams now, how can Greg? I can't think straight and I'm only ... '

'I want you to promise me something, darling,' Mum said firmly. 'That you won't let some ... some misplaced sense of guilt let you ... stop revising.'

'I can't,' I wailed. 'I can't think about work now. I can't read that book, even.'

'Of course you can't,' she said. 'Not now. But when you've slept, you can. Everything will shift. You'll have to make yourself just cut off, and work. And somehow you've got to persuade Val that she must, too.'

'What does it matter, now? What does all that matter?'

She got hold of my hands. 'Colette, listen to me. It will help. It will help the pair of you. It'll be something to focus on, something separate.'

I collapsed back onto the bed and she pulled the covers round me. 'You're strong enough,' she said. 'I wouldn't be saying this to you if I didn't know that. Val will get through this. I promise you. And I'm here. I'll be here.'

Twenty-three

Ian had bribed Art into agreeing to go to a big family party on Sunday. Art had asked me along too, and I'd said I could only go if I got enough work done in the week. So it was pretty simple to phone and apologise and say I had too much on to come.

'I do, too,' Art said. 'I'm only staying an hour or two. Just long enough to get fed. Maybe we can go out in the week?'

'Maybe,' I said.

He didn't ask me what the matter was, or tell me I sounded different. Perhaps he didn't notice anything.

Val wasn't at school on Monday. I got through the day like a zombie. Somehow, just like Mum had said, I managed to keep the part of my brain that was set aside for work functioning. I felt as though I was in a long tunnel with the exit sealed off. No escape; only one way forward.

That night, after supper, Greg phoned. He asked if he and Val could come round. I said of course, and he asked, 'Will your Mum be there?'

'If you want her to be,' I said.

When the four of us were seated round the kitchen table with mugs of coffee, Greg started to speak. 'Mrs Rowlands, thank you for ... you know. We can't tell Val's mum. And I haven't told my parents yet, but I'm prepared to, and I know they'll help if ... if ... '

'We can't decide,' said Val in a rush. 'We think one thing one minute, and another the next. I mean – what right have we to ... to kill it. But if I don't – I can forget university, and ... and anything like that ... I mean, I know I can still go, but with a baby, what chance have I ... ' She started crying. 'I can't look after a *baby*! What sort of life would it have?' Greg leaned over and put his arm round her shoulders and she gulped out, 'I thought I was miscarrying this morning. And I was so relieved. But I didn't. Oh, God. I don't know what to do. I don't know what to do.'

'Do you think it's wrong, Val?' Mum said, quietly. 'Do you think abortion is a sin?'

'I don't know. I didn't before. Not in theory. But now I ... '

'Now you're pregnant it's different.'

'Yes. Except – every moment, I'm praying to see blood. I just want it to end.'

There was a silence. 'I don't think it's wrong,' croaked Greg. 'But it's Val's decision. She knows that.'

'That doesn't *help*,' wailed Val. 'I can't decide all on my own!'

'But he's right, dear,' said Mum, patting her arm. 'It's

131

your decision.' Then she sat back and said, 'You know, in a way, I can relate to those views that say sex is there for the sole purpose of making babies. And interfering with that – in ANY way – is a sin.'

I gawped at her. 'Mum, you don't mean that. You don't mean you agree with banning contraception ... '

'I didn't say I agreed with it. But I can see its logic. Because where do you draw the line with contraception? Where does the moment of life start? At the moment of conception? Some people say the IUD works by stopping the fertilised egg embedding in the womb. Is that abortion? And a lot of fertilised eggs don't make it – they just fall through anyway. What's that? Babies dying? Surely not.'

Val shook her head. 'Mine's embedded, though, isn't it?'

'Yes, dear. Yes, it is. But a huge proportion of pregnancies fail in the first three months. Early miscarriages. Often, women don't know they're having one. They just think their period's late – and a bit heavier than normal, when it does come. The embryo just hasn't grown properly. It's Nature's way.'

Val sighed. 'I wish that would happen to me.'

'If you mean that, Val,' said Greg urgently, 'if you really mean that, I think you should get rid of it. It's worse to bring an unwanted kid into the world than ... ' He tailed off.

'Abortion is legal up to a certain date, and illegal afterwards,' said Mum gently. 'And with good reason. At a certain point, that group of dividing cells inside you will – probably – become a baby. For what it's worth, Val, I don't believe it's one yet. And I don't believe it's wrong

132

to stop that process now. Although I know a lot of people do.'

Val looked at her, desperate, pleading.

'And for what it's worth, Val,' Mum went on, 'I had to make this decision myself, too. Five years ago.'

There was a deep shift in the room. Val and Greg both stared at Mum. Then they turned and looked at me, to see if I'd known.

I hadn't. I hadn't known a thing.

Mum put her hand over mine. Her face had gone kind of rigid. 'I'm sorry to just ... announce it like this, dear,' she said. 'But it might help Val to know someone else has been through it ...'

My mind was reeling. Five years ago. I'd been eleven, twelve. Mum had been forty-two. That's not too late to have a baby.'

'Why, Mum,' I croaked. 'Why didn't you have it?'

'Oh, it was a horrible decision. Dad and I cried over it, for weeks. The worst part was knowing it would have been your little brother or sister – yours and Sarah's – I mean, it was like getting rid of another of you.'

Yes, I thought. It was like that. It was that.

'But I was over forty, and overweight, and that's a big health risk, and I didn't want to put our family life in jeopardy. But most of all – I just didn't want another baby. Not like I'd wanted you and Sarah.'

'But did that give you the right to ...' I felt choked. I didn't know what I thought.

'I believe it did. I believe I had that right. And I haven't regretted it. Oh. I've had *regrets* – I've felt sad, and guilty, and I've had dreams – I still dream about it. But I've always known I'd do the same again.'

133

'But I'm not a health risk,' croaked Val. 'I'm young.'

Mum started to stroke her hair. 'But there are other reasons for you not to have a baby, Val. Your whole life is ahead of you. You're *so* young.'

Val collapsed down on the table and started crying again. Greg looked frozen, unable to move, unable to comfort her.

'I'd give anything for this not to have happened to you, Val,' Mum said. 'Anything.'

Mum came up to my room again that night, and sat on the bed. 'You blame me, don't you,' she said.

I looked at her, and shook my head. 'No,' I said. 'I mean – it felt weird when you told me. Like it could have been me, or something. Oh, God, I don't know.'

'It would have torn us all apart you know,' she said. 'Even if everything had gone fine. A new baby would have exhausted me, I'd have had no time for anything else. No time for you or Sarah. I remember looking at you – puberty had hit and you were all curvy and lovely, starting to look like a woman. And I thought: it's her turn now. My time for babies is over. As insane as this sounds right now, I was looking forward to being a grandma.' She took my hand. 'Just not yet, darling. Not for a long time yet.'

'I had no idea,' I said. 'No idea it was going on.'

'Why should you?'

'Was it awful? You know – having it done ... '

'Well, it wasn't exactly pleasant. But the operation was nothing compared to what we went through before, having to decide.'

I looked at her. I couldn't judge her. She hadn't judged Val. This is no time for judgements, I thought.

I just felt so sorry, about everything.

Twenty-four

Twenty-four

That Thursday I told Art I had to speak to him. I told him
I couldn't talk on the phone. We met at a pub half way
between our homes, and I told him what had happened.
I tried not to hate him for the relief which played very
clearly across his face when he realised the problem was
Val's, not mine.

'That's awful,' he said. 'Jesus, Coll, you scared me on the
phone. I wondered what was up.'

'This is up,' I said coldly.

'How could they be that dumb?' he went on.
'Withdrawal. Jesus.'

'Well – not everyone's as ... clued up as you.'

'She must want to kill him.'

'God, he didn't force her into it. It's just – it's so awful.
She doesn't know what she's going to do yet, and – '

'Well, won't she ... she'll get rid of it, won't she?'

136

'I think so. I don't know.'

'She can't want to go through with it! Saddled with a kid! I can't see Val as a single mum.'

'Why d'you assume she'd be single?'

'Well, they're hardly going to get married, are they? At seventeen?'

'All that – doesn't matter! Val has a *baby* growing inside her – she's got to decide whether to keep it or not!'

'Yeah, but she's got to think about the future. It's her life – Greg's life. It would really screw it up.'

'Look – it's not – not a mental thing. She can't sit down and draw up a list of pros and cons, and decide what's most *sensible*. She's really messed up!'

'But she'll feel better when she decides ...'

'Oh – you think so? It's that easy, is it? Suppose she makes the wrong decision?'

'Coll calm down. Why are you getting at me? It's not my fault.'

I fell silent. I was nearly in tears.

I said I had to get back fairly soon after that. I was very distant when we said good night, and he wasn't stupid enough to push it.

'Look – I'll phone you tomorrow,' he said. 'See how you are. Try not to worry, Coll.'

Val came round to see me two days later, white-faced and determined. She'd been to the doctor. She'd decided. She'd made an appointment at an abortion clinic because she couldn't bear the thought of being on a NHS waiting list. Between them, she and Greg had got together the money that was needed. Neither of them had told their parents.

'The appointment is for the end of the week. I have to go along and get two doctors to agree that I can have it done,' she said. Then she twisted her hands together and said, 'Coll – will you come along with me?'

'Me? But what about Greg ... ?'

'I don't want him to come.' Her face crumpled. 'We had a horrible row. I blame him, Coll – I can't help it. He told me he'd be careful. I keep hearing him say – I'll be careful.'

'Oh, Val.'

'And I hate him for – for not letting it get to him. He's still working – really hard. He says it helps, but Jesus, I can't work. I'm going to screw everything up because I've got all ... this to go through. It's not fucking *fair*. I feel he's abandoned me.'

'Oh, Val, you know that's not true. You know how upset he is.'

'Yes, but he's not the one going through it. He's not the one who's got to go through it. I hate him for it.'

I didn't know what to say. There wasn't any point in trying to get her to forgive Greg. She was in no state to forgive anyone.

We went to the clinic at Friday lunchtime. It wasn't a problem, skipping the afternoon study period at school. The clinic was only a short bus ride away – a huge old Edwardian house with a new extension at the side, where the outpatients section was. We were shown into the waiting room, and we huddled together in the corner. I could hear Val breathing quickly, shakily, beside me, and I reached out and nervously squeezed her hand.

There were about ten people in the waiting room, most in couples of some kind. As I looked around I realised that Mum must have waited in a room like this five years ago, but that thought was too awful to stay with for long. There were only two men, wearing the frightened, defiant faces of men in the enemy camp, hoping for tolerance, prepared for abuse. One of them was holding the hand of a pasty-looking blonde girl. She was wearing an engagement ring. So this baby wanted to come along too soon, I thought. Would they still get married after this, with all the pomp and frills? How long would they wait? Would there be other children, arriving the right side of the ceremony, and would there always be the shadow of the first child there, the one they'd turned away?

No one met anyone's eyes for long. There were two girls of about our age there, no, younger, both with their mothers. One mother was pale, with neat hair, conventionally dressed. And so sad. 'This isn't what I'd hoped for her,' her face seemed to say. 'This isn't how it was meant to be.' Her daughter looked neat, like her mother, and vacant, as though she'd gone somewhere else.

The other mother had dyed blonde hair, tight jeans, big earrings and a hard, coping kind of face. Her daughter, fifteen or so, half lay across the seats, sullen, withdrawn. They looked as though they'd been arguing before they got here, but all the same I thought I'd rather have her than the other mother. She looked like she'd be more support.

Above us, on the wall, the TV softly blared, locking into the captive daytime audience of women-at-home with kids. Advert after advert for baby food, nappies, creams. Babies rolled and chuckled and gurgled across the screen. It was horrible.

After ten minutes or so, Val's name was called. I stood up with her, uncertain.

'Your friend can come too, dear,' the nurse said. 'If you like.'

Val nodded. Her eyes were wide now with tension, apprehension. We were shown into a small office where a woman of about sixty with white hair in a bun was sitting behind a desk. She looked up as we came in, unsmiling.

'Come in, girls,' she said. 'Sit down. Now – which one of you is it?'

I was tense as anything as Val started to explain what had happened. I was waiting for the old woman to say something critical, something to upset Val. And then I was going to – I don't know. I felt so protective of Val as we sat there on the edge of our seats.

'We do a urine test – we have to assure ourselves you actually are pregnant,' the woman was saying. 'Then you see another doctor, and our counsellor, just to have a chat. It's a very emotional decision, as you know. We need to make sure it's the right thing.'

'It is,' said Val, white-faced. 'I know it is.'

'Yes, my dear, I think it is for you.'

Val seemed to melt. 'I just feel so *guilty*,' she wailed. 'I'm scared I'll regret it, never get over it ... you read all this stuff about how wrong it is, all those groups protesting in America ... '

'I've been practising since the fifties,' the woman interrupted, kindly. 'Long before abortion was legal. I used to see lines of women who'd "slipped up" – depressed, resentful – all so sad. All we could do was tell them to try and get on with it, they'd love the baby when it was here. I used to wonder if they did love their babies. It's different now. In this day and age, there's only one reason to have a baby. If you want one.'

Val was examined, and had blood and urine tests, and saw another doctor, and then she went in on her own to talk to the counsellor. When she came out, she looked as though she'd been crying, and the counsellor gave her shoulders a squeeze and said, 'Remember, phone me. When you want to.' Then Val had to make an appointment for the actual operation at the desk, and it was over. We walked down the road together, and found a grubby little café, and went in to get a coffee.

'The counsellor was very good,' Val whispered. 'She told me not to worry about hating Greg. She said it was normal.'

'Did it make you feel – did you still feel – you're doing the right thing?'

'Yes. She listened, mainly. She said the motto of the clinic was that every child should be a wanted child, which isn't always the same as a planned child – but – but I knew I didn't want this one.'

We sat quietly for a minute, then Val said, 'Coll ... I feel like I'm shutting things out. I feel like I've got to go ahead and do this, whatever the consequences afterwards. It's like – evil both ways. I've just got to do it.'

I felt scared when she said that. But I just rubbed her arm and said, 'Yes. You've made the right decision, Val.'

We didn't really talk much after that. It was as if a cold hand had come out from somewhere hidden and taken hold of us. And we knew that that lost, cold place was there all the time, no matter how much you tried not to think of it, and it was mostly luck whether you fell into it or not. This time, Val hadn't had the luck. Mum hadn't had it five years ago. Both of them would carry the weight of it with them, all their lives. I felt as if I was carrying it too.

Twenty-five

I saw Art on Saturday. He wanted me to come round but I said no, I wanted to meet in a pub. Neutral ground.

Art looked relieved when I told him Val had booked into the clinic. 'Thank God she's being sensible,' he said.

'I don't think *sense* comes into it,' I snapped. 'It's just – it's what she feels she has to do.'

'Yeah. This time next week it'll all be over.'

'Art – *Jesus*. It's not like having a *tooth* out. She feels terrible about it. She's got to live with it. I'm scared – I'm scared she'll regret it. I don't know what to say to her.'

Art put his hands above his head and stretched, a long, muscle-crunching stretch, and then he sighed. 'Look, Coll,' he said. 'I think you're great the way you've come through for Val. You'll help her get over it. I mean – things like that happen. You just have to get on with it.'

I stared down at the table. The cold hand wasn't real for

him. It hadn't touched him. It hadn't even brushed past his skin.

A bit later that evening I said, 'Art. Don't take this the wrong way. But there's less than two weeks now, until your exams. I think we should stop seeing each other. Until afterwards.'

He stared at me. 'What? *Why*?'

'This stuff with Val it's – I can't think straight. She needs my help. And I feel – I don't want to mess you up. I just – I think we should both just get through our exams. I don't want anything else going on.'

'Oh, terrific. You don't want me going on, you mean.'

'Art, don't get like that. You don't understand. I feel – wiped out. I don't want to mess you up.'

'You're mad. Why will you mess me up?'

'If we don't see each other, we can just get our heads down. I feel so screwed up about this and I – don't *want* to see you when I'm like this. I feel like shit. I just want it all to be over.'

And I'm afraid, I said inside my head. I'm afraid of everything. I'm afraid of what sex can do to you. I'm afraid of how much I feel for you. I'm afraid of not being able to control it any more. I'm afraid of spilling it out all over you, just before your exams.

I'm afraid you don't feel the same for me.

'Please try to understand,' I said, weakly.

'All right,' he said finally. 'Shut yourself away. I'll pretend you don't exist. For four weeks.'

'Don't phone me, either,' I said. 'If you say you're going to phone, I'll – I'll be hoping you do, and if I hear your voice, I'll want to see you, and if ...'

I'd started to cry. He took my face in his hands and

pressed his forehead against mine. 'Four weeks, then,' he said. 'If it's really what you want. Maybe you're right. For four weeks I'll just – work.'

At the end of the evening, as he walked away, I felt a great jolt of panic. I can't do it, I thought. I can't have no contact with him at all. I need to see him. I need to know what he's doing.

Then I made myself go in the house.

The countdown had started.

Twenty-six

I wasn't involved in getting Val to the clinic, or picking her up afterwards. Greg did that. She'd calmed down about him.

She came to stay at my house right afterwards. We were all on study leave now, and she told her mum we were going to do some work together, and if she stayed the night we could have a laugh after we'd worked.

Val's mum believed her.

'The worst bit,' said Val, 'was being wheeled into the operating theatre. You have to walk down there, and then you get on a trolley and they put this thing in your hand to knock you out. I was going under, but I wasn't quite out, and they wheeled me through these horrible plastic curtains. It was like – it was like a ghost train – you know, when you clatter through those little doors? I wanted to scream. Then I came round, and it was over, but I didn't realise it. I kept trying to tell them I was awake – I thought they hadn't done it yet – I was all muddled – I thought I'd be awake for the operation. Then this nurse told me it was over. And I felt so relieved, Coll. Five minutes later I puked up, but I didn't care. I felt so relieved it was over.'

Greg called back a few hours later. He'd bought some flowers. I wasn't sure how well they'd go down, but I suppose he thought he ought to bring something. I left the two of them alone in my room. I could hear crying, at one point – I think it was Greg.

And then he left and, amazingly, we got down to some work. Val said her head was quite clear, and she had energy, and she started reading through her files, jotting down notes.

At night I put Val into my bed. I blew up the air mattress for myself, and put it alongside her, and we slept.

After that, Val often came over and worked alongside me. She made me think of soldiers in a war zone. All right once the battle's still on, it's when they get home, when they're safe, that the nightmares start. Well, the battle was still on for Val. She was steely, determined to survive. And we worked.

We didn't speak much about the abortion, but I knew one of the reasons she wanted to come and work in my room was to be with someone who knew what she'd been through. I admired the way she grafted on. Every now and then I'd see her gazing into space, and when she saw me looking, she'd smile at me.

Mum was encouraging and supportive and kept us supplied with nourishing snacks. We were like a couple of nuns, hair scraped back, clothes simple, dedicated to

147

our task. We didn't expect to feel happy, so when we had a laugh or enjoyed a chat together, it was like a bonus. In an odd way, it wasn't a bad time.

Missing Art would catch me unawares, though. I'd be showering or something and I'd suddenly feel this ache, this longing, so strong it was like the breath had been knocked out of me. I'd wash my hair and look in the mirror and feel so empty; I'd want to get dolled up and go out with him and have fun; I'd want to paint my nails, do my eyes and show off, I'd want Art to look at me and want me. I was sick of being shut away.

I wondered how he was doing, how he was coping. I'd regret not trusting myself; not being the wonderful, supportive girlfriend, helping him through his exams. And several times, bad times, I pictured Art going out on the pick-up, or giving someone like Sally a ring, out of sheer spite. But I wouldn't let myself phone him.

Then, one morning, there was a letter for me.

I recognised Art's odd, sloping writing immediately. I felt something like terror as I picked it up off the mat. What on earth had he written? Get lost? Goodbye? I ripped open the envelope, and read:

Hi, swot, how's it going?

You didn't say anything about not writing, so I am. Hope Val's OK.

Ten days and it'll all be over. My first exam is Monday and I almost think I'm ready. I've been working OK. Maybe it was a good idea of yours, not seeing each other, but it's hard to get to sleep at night.

Too much brain activity, not enough physical. I went swimming on Thursday, but you weren't there. I miss you. See you in two weeks.

Love, Art.
PS Is it against the rules for you to write back?

I don't suppose many people would call that a love letter, but it was for me. I smiled to myself all morning as I thought of him going swimming in the hope of seeing me. Then I let myself write to him. It went to three drafts.

Dear Art,

I'm so glad you've been working OK. You'll do brilliantly, I know you will. You really wouldn't have wanted me around these last weeks. I felt so messed up about Val. I'm sorry I wasn't at the pool.

Everything went OK for Val. She's working away now, very determined. She's made me work harder. I've finished my course work. End-of-term exams start next Wednesday.

I can't wait to see you after all this is over. I miss you, too.

Love, Coll.
PS Don't write back, OK? I don't want to expect anything.
PPS GOOD LUCK!

I hadn't put in all I wanted to say – I hadn't said that it's unreal that I can't be with you, it's like being starved ... I see you sometimes when I shut my eyes, and it's like I can smell you, your skin, your closeness. I hadn't said I think I'll go mad if I don't hold you soon.

Twenty-seven

The first day of the exams arrived. I was pretty calm. I knew that unless the paper was a real blitzer, I'd be OK. And after what Val had been through, and survived, exams didn't seem so major. The trick was to keep it all in perspective.

I saw Val, just as we went into the hall. She looked scared but focused. I got hold of both her hands and squeezed them. 'Good luck,' I said. 'You deserve it.'

'So do you, Coll,' she answered. 'Good luck.'

And it went OK. I didn't panic when I read the questions; I made notes; I kept an eye on the time, dividing it up between the questions. I read my answers through afterwards, fixing the spelling and grammar. These are just practice shots anyway, I thought. Not like Art, doing the real thing.

We had ten days of exams, and study time in between.

151

If more than a day went by without seeing Val I'd phone her, just to check on her. And then the exams finished, and even though it wasn't the end of term, we felt we were free.

There were two more days before Art's final exam. I wanted to call him, but I kept to our pact. The first night I went to the Dog and Duck with everyone. Val got roaring drunk – absolutely legless. Greg's exams were still going on but he turned up at the pub at about ten-thirty and drove her home. It was good to see them together again.

The next night, I got a couple of videos out, and I ate chocolate. I couldn't sleep. Tomorrow afternoon, Art would finish. Art would be free.

I went for a long run the next morning. And then I made a very large, fruit-packed breakfast for myself and ate it slowly, tasting every mouthful. Then I locked myself in the bathroom.

I showered and shampooed and tweezered. I kept looking down at my body and admiring it, enjoying it as though it hadn't been around for a while. I transformed my raggy nails with an emery board. I was starting to feel nervous. It was over four weeks since I'd seen Art, since I'd even talked to him.

I outlined my eyes with a kohl crayon and mascara, and I put on my new top, the one Art liked, and some shorts. My legs were just beginning to get brown.

Midday was the time Art's last exam ended. If I went round to his house, I might meet him there ...

No one answered my knock. I hung around outside his front gate for a while beginning to regret just turning up like this. I should have waited at home, and phoned.

Waited at home? Who was I kidding?

I walked down the path, thinking maybe I'd wander along in the direction of his school. Then I heard yelling, chanting, the sort you hear from football hooligans, coming this way. I sat on the wall to wait. Half a dozen lads surged round the corner, jumping about, shouting. It wasn't football sending them screwy, it was the end of exams. The end of school, for ever. I recognised Art, even from that distance. He had a great walk. Just enough swagger in it. He looked as though he really fitted his skin.

I had a lump in my throat so big I was ashamed. I got down from the wall and stood there and watched him as he got closer, closer, and then he stopped, half way down the road, and shouted 'Coll?'

I waved, jerkily. He came closer, almost running, not quite, while his friends whistled behind him, and then he stopped in front of me.

'Hi, Coll,' he said.

'Hi,' I croaked. 'How did it go?'

His face kind of twisted up then, and we sort of rushed at each other. It was some impact. You know when Superman catches Lois Lane during a headlong plunge? It was that kind of impact. And we just held each other – we didn't even kiss.

The friends drew alongside. 'Oh, for fuck's sake, Johnson,' one said. 'I thought we were going to the pub.'

'Come on you bastard,' said another. 'Put her down.'

Art had buried his face in my hair. I could feel his warmth all round me.

'Come on, for Christ's sake. She can come too.'

Art glanced up. 'Look – I'll see you there,' he muttered.

153

'OK? We'll come along later.'

There was a great jeering outcry at this, and a load of obscene comments, but we didn't care, we were already halfway up his front path.

My throat still felt frozen, as we shut the door behind us. Art wasn't speaking, either. His eyes looked wet, but then everything I looked at was sort of swimming.

'Do you ... do you want some lunch?' he said. I shook my head and got hold of him, and we started kissing, and climbed slowly upstairs, still kissing.

'So, weren't you going to phone me? When you'd finished?' I said, as we got to his room.

'Yes. From the pub. I got kind of swept along with those guys. And I was ...'

'What?'

'I don't know. I felt like my brain was disintegrating. I wanted a drink. That last exam sucked. You look beautiful.'

We undressed each other, and let it all happen, and when I came, I cried, I couldn't help myself.

We lay wrapped up together on the bed. After a while, Art said, 'Thank God it's all over.'

'How well d'you think you did?'

'Maybe OK. That last one was the real screw-up. Coll?'

'What?'

'I did some thinking. I mean – you were upset about Val, and I think I was a bit of a jerk. Was that why you –'

' – wanted a break? Oh, Art, no. I just – I felt I was falling apart, and I didn't want to land that on you when you were working, and I had to get myself together to work too ...'

'Only ... I think I was a bit insensitive.'

'Insensitive? You? Never ... ' And then I stopped, because the lump had come back to my throat. I hugged him so hard he grunted in protest.

'I think Val's all right,' I said. 'I think it'll be OK. I mean – it's not the sort of thing you ever forget, but ... '

He was playing with my hair, twisting it round his hand. 'I don't know what I'd do if it happened to you,' he said.

We stayed on the bed, just locked together. 'Thanks for your letter,' he said after a while. 'And the orders not to write another one. You mean cow.'

'Art – you'd've stopped me focusing. I mean – look at us. Would this have fitted in with exam revision?'

'Yes. I'm focused,' he said. 'I'm *really* focused.'

'Not in your brain, you're not.'

'Sod my brain. Those three weeks were very bad for me. I had to recycle all that sperm.'

'You had to -? Oh, shut up.'

'No contact – just one poxy letter. I nearly sent you a fax after that. Through your dad's machine. Just to wind you up.'

'You should've done.'

'I wondered about his computer, too. Leaving you dirty messages on e-mail. Has he got e-mail?'

'No.'

'Pity. We could've got it on over the Internet.'

I laughed. 'Yeah. Cybersex. We could've done. Trouble is, you're nearly illiterate. I doubt if I'd have even got turned on ... whereas *you* ... '

'All right, Ms Literary Genius. I wouldn't have got turned on either. Words on a screen instead of this. Do me a favour.'

He'd started stroking me, from the shoulder to the leg, very slowly. 'Do you know what people who have cybersex are called?' he asked.

'No. Tell me.'

'Pathetic bastards.'

Later, we got dressed. 'Let's go to the pub,' I said. 'You told your friends you would.'

He screwed up his nose. 'D'you really want to?'

'Well - it's the big celebration, isn't it? The finish? You shouldn't miss that. The last time you're all little school-boys together. Will it matter if I'm there?'

He smiled at me. 'It'll matter if you're not,' he said.

Twenty-eight

The pub was packed, in uproar. The landlord had a tense, fixed smile on his face, glad for all the money pouring in from the private school sixth-formers, but secretly hating the lot of them. When they spotted us, Art's friends ran through the usual collection of obscene comments on what we'd been up to, and Mark stood up and offered to buy us a drink. He seemed completely ratted already. He took his school tie off, and looped it round my neck. 'I shan't need that EVER again,' he announced, breathing beer fumes into my face. 'You can have it! Sally doesn't want it!'

'One of the reasons I'm so glad it's all over,' muttered Art, 'is I shan't have to see this lot every day.'

I didn't care about the rude comments, or the tie, or anything. I suddenly felt wild – fantastic. I was with Art again. I sat as close to him as I could get and let happiness fill every part of me.

I got bought so many drinks I lost count. Art was knocking it back too. 'We'll regret this later,' I said.

'I don't care. It's the end. I can't believe it.'

And I didn't care. I suddenly didn't care about anything. I wanted a break from feeling so much, so intensely. I put my arm round Art's neck, and picked up another glass.

Later, when I was fighting my way back from the loo, I collided with Art's ex-best friend Joe.

I did a double-take, and he staggered sideways and said, slurringly, 'Hello, Coll!'

'Hi,' I said. 'I didn't think you went to Art's school.'

'I don't. He left our place after GCSEs. We've just finished, too. There's a *helluva* lot of us here.'

'Do they all hate him as well?'

'What?'

'He told me you still hate him. For not doing a better job of fighting off your girlfriend. If you want my opinion, you're an unforgiving sod.'

Joe laughed, scenting battle. 'I don't want your opinion.'

'Look Joe, at that party, you seemed like a really intelligent bloke. Not the sort to sulk for ever and ever over some silly *mistake*.'

'And you seemed like all the other girls who've gone gaga over that shit. You'd stick up for him whatever he did.'

'Oh no I wouldn't. All I did was give him a second chance. And now it's working for us. It's really working.'

'Oh, yeah?' he sneered, and motioned with his head over to where Art was sitting.

With Sally on his lap.

'Oh, *bollocks*,' I erupted. I stormed over to them.

'Get off, Sal,' said Art.

'Oh Art, we're just having a cuddle!' complained Sally. 'You're not jealous, are you, Colette? Go and have a smooch with Mark. I won't mind!'

'Well *I'd* mind,' I spat. 'I'd sooner have all my teeth pulled out.'

The table erupted with laughter, and Sally stood up huffily.

'Joe's over there,' I said. 'I was trying to convince him you're not a complete lowlife. I look round, and there you are making it with ... '

'Coll, I was being harassed. Sal, tell her you were harassing me.'

'Piss *off*,' I said, then I turned on my heel and walked unsteadily back to Joe. He came to meet me, grabbed me by the shoulders and plastered his lips on my mouth.

He'd reckoned without the automatic reaction of the Woman Trained in Self Defence. I kneed him. Not enough to make him collapse on the floor, just enough to make him back off. Fast.

'Jesus *Christ*! You all right?' Art was behind me, sounding half-appalled, half-impressed. 'Coll – you've crippled him. Look – he can't move. She's dangerous. She's lethal. I should've warned you.'

'Joe was making a stupid *point*,' I said. 'He wanted to show you what it felt like to see your friend get off with your girlfriend.'

'I think I'm going to throw up ... ' groaned Joe.

'The difference *being*,' I ranted on, 'that I didn't want to get off with *you*. That's the thing you won't face – your

159

poxy ex-girlfriend made the moves. And Art's a real slag. He wouldn't have been able to resist. You just can't say no, can you, Art? Not even to complete sharons like Sally.'

There was a silence. Oh, God, I thought, hazily. What did I just do? What did I just *say*? Then I heard Joe laughing. At first I thought he was puking, but I realised it was laughter. And then the landlord appeared at my shoulder and said, 'Are these young men bothering you, Miss?' And Art said, 'No. She's bothering us.' And then *he* started to laugh. And my legs suddenly gave in to gravity and I slithered down and sat on the floor. 'Oh, I'm terribly sorry,' I announced. 'They've just finished their exams.'

'Perhaps you've all done enough celebrating, now,' the landlord said, pulling me to my feet. 'Perhaps you'd better go home.'

The three of us wove out of the pub together. 'I wasn't making a point, Coll,' Joe said plaintively. 'I fancy you.'

'That's the trouble,' groaned Art. 'We fancy the same people.'

'That's no excuse,' I said. 'Where are we going?' I'd somehow got in the middle and they were both leaning on me as we lurched along the road.

'I'm not a slag, Coll,' moaned Art. 'I'm not.'

'You are, mate,' said Joe. 'You really are. A slag.'

'But it was *her* fault.'

'There you go *again*!' I said. 'Blaming other *people*!'

'Hit him, Coll,' said Joe. 'Go on. Hit him.'

Somehow, we steered our way back to Art's house, staggered through the door and into the living room. 'I think you're great, Coll,' Joe was saying. 'I know you think I'm only saying this because I'm drunk but I think you're great.' Then he lay down on the carpet and went to sleep.

'Art, get me some water,' I moaned.

'Of course, Coll. Anything. Anything you want,' he said, then he fell face first onto a sofa.

I went into the kitchen, filled a pint mug of water, and drank it. Then I went back to the living room and collapsed on the other sofa.

'Oh, terrific. The end of exams, I take it?'

I peered blearily across the room. It was almost dark. Ian was standing in the doorway, in an intimidating smart suit.

'Hello, Mr Johnson,' I whispered. 'Sorry.'

'Colette, there seem to be two young men stretched out in here.'

'One of them's Joe.'

Ian disappeared. Minutes later he was back, bearing three glasses of fizzy, milky-looking stuff. 'This is my hangover cocktail,' he said, walking over to me and kicking Joe gently as he passed. 'It never fails. Knock it back.'

'Oh, thank you. Thank you that's really kind.' I swallowed it gratefully. I trusted it.

'Joe – Art – come on lads. Drink this.' Joe reared up bleary-eyed and Ian handed him a glass.

I took the third glass from Ian and went to sit beside Art with it. Ian smiled, and left.

'Why did we *do* that?' I groaned. 'Why did we do that to our bodies? I feel awful. Art, wake up.'

'He's probably dead,' Joe moaned, softly.

I was stroking Art's hair back from his face. 'Come on,

I said. 'Drink this.'

'Stop smiling at him. You can't fancy him in that state.'

'Yes, she does,' Art croaked out. 'You do, don't you, Coll?'

'No. You're revolting. Drink this.'

The three of us sat on the floor in the half light, drinking water, bonded by how terrible we felt.

'It's a time for forgiveness, Joe,' I said, in a singsong voice. 'Time to forgive the terrible betrayal of your lowlife friend.'

'Shut up, Coll,' muttered Art.

'After a suitable period of penance, of course,' I went on. 'After he's crawled on his knees all the way to – '

'Shut *up*, Coll,' said Art.

'You're right,' announced Joe. 'It is time. I officially forgive you, you slag. But if you *ever*, ever do anything like that again ... '

'If I'm still around,' I assured him, 'I'll help you take him apart. Bit by bit. Then we can eat him.'

Art was smirking. 'I like jealous women,' he said. 'They're kind of passionate, they're ... '

'Spare us, Art,' I said.

'I might forgive you, Johnson, but I still hate you,' groaned Joe. 'You get all the girls. And I never get to meet any. I want someone for the summer. I want to fall in LURV. Coll—ditch him. Run away with me.'

'OK,' I said.

'I'll treat you right. I'll buy you flowers. I'll get your name tattooed on my face. I'll drink champagne out of your belly button – '

'Is that meant to be good?' said Art, looking interested.

'You *see*? He's a swine. He has no originality. No romance.'

'Joe, listen,' I said. 'I've just had a brainwave.'

'Oh, God,' muttered Art.

'I'm going to introduce you to Rachel. I think you'd really get on.'

'Who's Rachel?' asked Joe.

'One of Coll's mates,' said Art. 'Pretty. Small, quiet. Really bright eyes.'

'You make her sound like a fieldmouse. She's shy, but she's great when you get to know her. And she doesn't like Art.'

'Yes she does.'

'No she doesn't. She thinks you're hard-looking. She told Val.'

'She's got taste then,' mused Joe. 'Could be my sort.'

'I will – engineer it,' I announced. 'I'll — I'll have you all round to eat. Celebrate the end of term. Mum won't mind. And I'll ask Val and Greg.'

'Oh God, *no*,' moaned Art. 'Please.'

'Last time Val saw Art,' I explained, 'she smacked him in the face.'

'This is sounding better and better,' said Joe. 'When's it going to be?'

Joe limped off home not long afterwards. Art and I stayed hunched up in the gloom together. We were beginning to feel human again.

'They're over, Coll,' Art said. 'I'm a grown up.'

'Sure you are.'

'All I have to do is wait for the results and then ... '

' ... go away to college.'

In the silence, he reached out and got hold of my

hand. I sat and stared at the floor. I hadn't given the future much consideration. But it was true. He was going away, and I was staying here.

I can't bear it, I thought. We've got no future together and I can't bear it. This thing we've grown together, this passion we have, this love – it'll die. We won't just abandon it or throw it out, like Fran did that cheese plant, the one that Art rescued. But it'll die. It'll have no water, no food. No light.

It'll die.

Twenty-nine

This idea of having everyone round for dinner got fixed in my mind. It was symbolic for me. Now all the drama was over, I didn't just want to wind down, I wanted to wind up. This party was going to heal friendships, cement friendships, make friendships – it was going to be great.

Mum was scathing, of course. A DINNER party? Oh, for heaven's sake. How very pretentious.'

'Just a casserole or something. Something different to sending out for pizza. I thought you'd approve.'

'I shall do better than approve. I shall keep out of the way. Completely out of the way, until it's over and you've cleared up.'

'You mean you won't help me cook it ... ?'

'Correct. In fact, you can make enough to give Dad, Sarah and me some first, as a thank you for letting you colonise the kitchen all night ... '

Fran, by contrast, oozed enthusiasm for the plan.

'What menu are you thinking of?' she asked.

'Menu? Er – just a big stew, I thought.'

'Very practical, darling. A summer stew. With lots of rough peasant red. I'll give Art a few bottles.'

'Oh, Fran, that's great!'

'And would you … would you like me to knock up a pudding for you all? I love making puddings.'

I looked at her coy, hopeful face and said, 'Fran, that would be brilliant. Absolutely brilliant.'

I decided on eight of us. Val and Greg, me and Art, Caro and Dave, and Joe and Rachel. Caro and Dave weren't exactly a couple, so my matchmaking intentions wouldn't look too obvious. I told Art we had to make sure Rachel and Joe sat together, because Rachel wasn't the sort to shout over the top of people.

'Not like you, you mean,' said Art.

'Oh, ha, ha. You like assertive women. You know you do.'

'I love 'em. And manipulative women.'

'I am not manipulative. I'm … creating an opportunity.'

On the evening of the dinner, Art arrived looking pained with a backpack full of bottles and a huge bowl full of creamy stuff with fancy chocolate scrapings on top.

'I had to *walk* here,' he complained. 'With this stupid gunk. For a poxy dinner party. You're as bad as Fran.'

'Oh, balls. It's not a dinner party. We're just having fun, sharing food, conversation … '

'Well, I'll sit through it, but tomorrow you've got to come out with me on the bikes and shag me in a wood somewhere.'

'Deal,' I said, praying Mum wasn't anywhere in earshot.

Art unloaded everything on the kitchen table. 'You know, I really like Fran,' I said as I inspected it. 'She's so kind.'

Art took a big breath and said, 'I think they're going to split up, Coll.'

'What?'

'Fran and Dad. She's talking of moving out. I don't know.'

'Oh – God. That's awful.'

'He's – I think he's got heavily involved with someone else. He's hardly been home. She can't hang around with that going on.'

I thought of my stolid, stable parents. 'What about you?' I asked.

He shrugged. 'What about me? When I get to college I'm out of it all anyway.'

I felt the coldness again, waiting. We were like children playing, before the real stuff started.

I shook the thoughts off and finished laying the table. The smell of my casserole was filling the room, deliciously. Art opened one of the bottles of wine and poured out two glasses. Before he could hand me one, I put my arms round him and hugged him. 'I'm bonkers about you,' I said recklessly.

'Bonkers. Cool word, Coll.'

'OK, passionate. I'm insane with passion about you.'

'Show me.'

I gave him a long, purposeful kiss. Then I said, 'Your turn.' He started to kiss me back, and I pulled away. 'No. Your turn to ... to *say* something.

'Words don't mean shit,' he said. 'People lie all the time.'

'I don't,' I answered.'I'm not lying.'

He smiled, and took a mouthful of wine.

'It *can* work out for people,' I said. 'Just because it's not worked out for your dad and Fran ... '

'Coll. Don't get so serious.'

'I want to be serious,' I said, and I suddenly felt scared – I could feel my heart beating. 'You going away to college – that's serious.'

'I don't want to think about it,' he replied. 'It's in the future.'

'Yes, but ... sometimes you have to think about the future, you have to face things – '

'Oh, come on, Coll. We've got the holidays first. You're still coming away with me, aren't you?'

I smiled, placated. 'Yes. 'Course I am. It's just – '

'Save it, Coll. Everyone'll be here in a minute.'

And then, on cue, the doorbell went.

'That'll be Val,' I said. 'I asked her to get here early ... '

'Let's hope it goes better than her birthday,' Art said.

I stared at him. 'Oh, God. Suppose it doesn't. What have I *done*?'

'Too late, kid,' he gloated. 'Too late.'

Thirty

Val and Greg were very stiff and polite at first. They handed Art a bottle of wine and accepted two glasses in return, Greg hovering over Val like an anxious husband. Then Rachel, Caro and Dave arrived and this time beer was exchanged. The conversation got going a little, but very stiffly. I began to wonder when Art would actually open his mouth to speak. He was still like an outcast. In desperation, I turned my cassette player up louder, but it didn't seem to help.

Ten long minutes later, the doorbell went again, and Joe bounded in, with some manic story about why he was late. He seemed genuinely pleased to be introduced to everyone, especially Rachel. He drew Art into the conversation, then he started insulting him so brilliantly that everyone laughed, even Art. Val was visibly thawing out. Greg joined in the conversation. His mind seemed to run on the same cracked tracks as Joe's. They sparked off each other and the stuff they started coming out with was hilarious.

'Time to eat,' I announced, heading for the oven. Everyone squeezed round the table, Rachel and Joe grabbing chairs next to each other as though they'd been primed. Well, Joe had been – but I was pleased by how keen Rachel seemed, too. Greg sat down next to Val and put his arm round her, and she turned to him and kissed him. Dave uncorked some more wine; Caro got busy handing round the baked potatoes. 'It's going to be OK,' I thought, as I started dishing out my stew. 'It's working out.'

As we were eating, everyone talking with their mouths full, the kitchen door opened a crack and then shut again, with a shriek of giggles. 'That's Sarah,' I groaned. 'She's got one of her horrible little friends to stay.' The second time the door creaked open I called out, 'Sarah – clear off.' The giggling got louder. The third time it opened, and stayed open, Art got to his feet. He went down on his knees, reached round the door, and caught Sarah by the arm.

'Hey, Sarah,' he said, smooth as butter. 'You're distracting us, OK? How about leaving us to it?'

Sarah gazed at him, all masochistic adoration. Then she melted away.

'Sarah's in love with Art,' I explained.

'Christ, another female with no taste,' said Joe. Val shrieked with laughter.

I refilled the plates until no one could eat any more. 'I think we should wait a bit before we launch into that,' I said, indicating Fran's pudding.

'I think we should boogie,' said Caro, getting to her feet.

There was a general groan round the table. Caro is famous for her love of dancing. She's really good, and she's known for going completely over the top on occasions. She turned up the tape and began jumping around. Yup, this was one of the occasions.

'All *right*,' said Joe, joining her. He was as bad as she was good. But it didn't matter. Soon we were all on our feet, swaying about, pausing every now and then to grab a drink. Joe had got hold of Rachel now, and was doing some kind of mad rock and roll.

'Come on, Art,' I said, 'I'm going to teach you to jive.'

'No chance,' he said, pushing me up against the wall and trying to get into a clinch. I shoved him backwards, laughing. 'I'm setting the atmosphere,' he said, 'for Joe and Rachel.'

Then I looked up over his shoulder, and there, surreally, was Mum's large back view at the sink. She was calmly filling the kettle. 'Just making some coffee,' she called out. 'You carry on.'

So we did.

The party didn't break up until after two. It couldn't have gone better. In among all the raving and jiving, Val had had a chat with Art, and almost apologised to him. Greg had had a slow, nostalgic dance with me. Caro had gone bananas, Dave had got happily drunk. And Joe and Rachel had ended up wound round each other in the corner, swapping phone numbers.

Then in the early hours, we'd all had Fran's pudding and some coffee, and everyone had left, leaving Art and me to clear up. We didn't mind. It was good to be alone again.

'I thought that went really well – ' I began.

'Here we go. Full smug mode.'

'Well, it *did*. You saw Joe and Rachel – '

'Yup. His tongue so far into her ear it was coming out the other side.'

'Oh, *please*!'

'Come on, start clearing. I'm knackered.'

I gathered up plates while Art tipped empty bottles noisily into a binbag, still discussing the party. Then suddenly Mum appeared in the doorway, in her terrifying green candlewick dressing gown.

'How are you getting home, young man?' she said sternly.

'Ah,' said Art. 'I … er … walked here. I'll call a cab … '

'It's nearly DAWN. You won't get one at this hour – not one that won't charge a king's ransom, anyway. You can stay. IN MY OFFICE.' And she turned on her heel.

When we'd finished in the kitchen we went upstairs. I got Art a duvet and a pillow, and we made up the bed settee by Mum's desk. Then we sat down on it together, and I nuzzled my face into his shirt. 'I love your smell,' I said dreamily. 'It's really bonding, the way people smell. I used to love the smell of our dog – she died last year.'

'Great. So I'm on a par with your dead dog. Who smelt best?'

'Don't be *stupid*. It's just – I used to lie next to her for ages with my head buried in her side, just breathing it in.'

'Hot, Coll. You are some hot – '

'Oh, shut up. Haven't you ever loved an animal? Have you kept a pet?'

'Turtles. I didn't love them and I sure as shit didn't go around *smelling* them.'

'You're really *limited*, you know that?'

'And you're a screaming pervert,' he said, and grabbed me, rolling me backwards onto the couch. 'Come on, Coll,' he murmured, 'get in bed with me.'

I looked at him, and then I looked round at the room that had so much of Mum in it she could have been in there with us and together we burst out laughing and said in unison, 'No'.

Thirty-one

Over the next few days Art had a lot on to do with leaving school. I hadn't officially broken up for the summer yet, either, and I had to put in a few appearances in the classroom. It wasn't until the end of that week that we arranged to meet up again.

It was a beautiful afternoon when I biked round to his house. It felt like the summer had really started. I rode along thinking happily about all the wonderful free time ahead of us and then, less happily, about how I could manage to persuade Mum that going away on holiday with Art was a good idea. Or how I could even manage to bring up the subject.

I shot down his road, smiling already with anticipation, drew up by his gate and saw three huge 'For Sale' signs in the front garden.

To me, they were as grim as gibbets. I dumped my

bike, raced up the front path and knocked.

Art opened the door. 'What's going on?' I wailed. 'What are those signs?'

He shrugged. 'I told you they were splitting up.'

'But – but – they're selling the *house*!' I pushed past him, into the hall. It was a scene of complete devastation. Pictures had been pulled down off the walls and stacked untidily on the floor; all the rugs were rolled up. I went through into the kitchen. Everything was being torn down. Boxes were everywhere, full of cooking stuff. And there, in the corner, half-swept up, was a heap of smashed crockery.

'Oh, Jesus,' I muttered. 'What's been happening?'

'Fran's going,' Art said, dully. 'That's her stuff she's packing up.'

'But the plates, over there – '

'She went ballistic last night. She smashed everything. They'd already put the house up for sale.'

'Oh, Art. Why didn't you *phone* me?'

'To say what?'

'But you're losing your *home*!'

'This isn't my home.'

'What are you going to do? What's going to happen?'

'Dad's getting a flat in London, near his office. I'll stay there when I need to.'

I felt stricken. This house was going, this place where we'd spent so much time together. Now when Art came back from college, in the holidays, he'd have nowhere to go. Not near me anyway.

'It's ... it's so *sudden*,' I said frantically. 'When will you move out?'

'I'm going to go away for as much of the summer as I

175

can,' he said. 'And then when I get back — I'll go to college.'

I could feel tears filling my eyes. He was talking as though I had nothing to do with it, as though I wasn't in the picture at all.

'Hey, Coll, what's wrong?' he said, walking over and putting his arms round me. 'You're going to come with me, aren't you?'

'Come with — where? For how long?' I wailed.

'I dunno. I've just got to get away, Coll.' Then he started kissing me, burying his face in my hair, and half lifting me off my feet. He felt frozen, kind of cold and hungry. 'Come on,' he said in a low voice. 'Let's go up to my room.'

The last thing I wanted to do then was make love. I was still too shocked by seeing his house up for sale, and all the sad signs of moving out inside. But I didn't have the heart to push him away. Soon we went upstairs and got undressed in silence, and got into bed together. He held on to me so tightly it felt almost desperate, as though all he wanted to do was lose himself.

Afterwards, he said, 'Don't move, Coll. Let's stay here for a while. Let's just stay here, wrapped up.'

I held him against me and tried to get him to talk about Fran and his dad splitting up, but he wouldn't. He started to outline his plans for the summer instead. 'Dad knows someone with a place in Greece,' he said. 'We could use it as a base. He's giving me a stack of money, Coll.' He laughed, sneering. 'Buying me off.'

'Art, I can't just go away for the whole summer. I mean — I'm not even sure I can go away with you at *all* —'

'Oh, Christ,' he exploded. 'You're going to have to

break away some time.'

Things happened very fast for Art over the next few days. Fran moved out completely; Ian went down to stay with his new girlfriend in London, and Art started this kind of camping existence in the half-empty house. I went round there every day, and we both acted as though it was great that we had the whole place to ourselves, but there was something terrifying about it. Estate agents would let themselves in and out of the place with no warning, to show potential buyers around.

When we heard people arrive we'd lock ourselves into his room and keep completely silent as they tried the door. They usually swore and said things like, 'Well luckily it's only one of the small bedrooms.' It should have been funny but it got to you after a while.

I was there once when Ian phoned up. Art was quite cool and capable on the phone, telling him he was all right, then afterwards he retreated right inside himself and bit my head off when I asked him what Ian had said.

We didn't go out much, despite the beautiful weather. We used up the tins of food in the cupboards and got lots of takeaways. A couple of times I tried to get him to come round to my house for a meal, but he refused. Twice we fought over me not asking Mum about going to Greece yet.

We made love a lot. There was a compulsive feeling to it now that depressed me a bit, as though he'd never be happy, never satisfied.

All I wanted to do was make him feel better, and I couldn't seem to. But I knew he wanted me there with him, I knew I was all he had now, and that was enough for me.

Well, almost enough. I longed for him to open up to me, tell me what he felt about me, but he was as closed down as he'd ever been. More, now this had happened. There was nothing I could do about it.

On Wednesday I left Art's place early and went into town with Val, shopping. We both said how good it was to be without blokes for a while. She told me how she was fed up with Greg treating her like china and how they hardly ever just had a laugh any more; I got the impression it wouldn't last a lot longer between them. She talked about how she still had these dreadful feelings of panic, about the abortion, about whether she'd done the wrong thing; but she said when she sat and thought quietly, she knew she'd do the same again. I was happy to listen and let her get things off her chest – I didn't really want to talk to her about what was happening with Art. I suppose I knew the dim view she'd take of it all.

I got back home at about five o'clock, walked into our kitchen, and stopped dead. Fran was sitting at the table with Mum, drinking tea, and my first, panic-filled thought was that she'd spilled everything about Art and me staying in the empty house together. I eyed Mum nervously, but I couldn't read anything in her face.

'Oh, there you are, Colette,' said Mum. 'Come and sit down with us.'

I joined them, warily, wondering how long Fran had been sitting there. They seemed very relaxed together, the two of them. It was bizarre.

Then Mum dropped her bombshell. 'Fran's been telling me about your idea of going to this little house in Greece,' she announced calmly. 'She was surprised I didn't know anything about it.'

'Oh,' I said, panicking all over again. 'Well, I – it's not definite – I mean – we've talked about it but – '

'It's Art who's dead set to go,' broke in Fran, diplomatically. 'Colette, darling, I've just been explaining ... everything ... to Justine. I mean – about Ian and me separating. Art's pretty upset about it all – well, *you* know. I've just been round there and he wouldn't talk to me – he – and Ian's never around to – ' she broke off and her mouth tightened, and Mum actually leaned over and squeezed her arm.

'I know how much Art wants to get away,' Fran went on. 'And it would do him so much good. I really just came round to assure your mum that – '

'It sounds the perfect set up,' interrupted Mum, firmly, amazingly. 'Fran's been telling me all about it. A beautiful village right by the sea with lots of people around to keep an eye on you both. And no rent. What an opportunity.'

It wasn't my mother speaking. It couldn't be.

'They just haven't got around to renting it out this summer,' said Fran. 'It's only tiny, quite primitive. Ian and I went ... the year before last, just for a week. And there will be people we know, staying in the houses nearby – your mum will be able to contact you, Colette ... '

'It's just a question of dates, then,' said Mum efficiently.

All I could do was goggle at Mum. She was practically packing my case for me.

'We can work out all the details later,' Fran said. 'Well – Art'll do it. He knows how to get there – he's been there before.' Then she checked her watch, exclaimed anxiously, and got up to go.

I followed her and at the door she put her arms round me and gave me a huge hug. 'I'm so glad Art's got *you*,

Colette,' she said. 'I'm ... I'm worried about him. He seemed so depressed when – '

'Yeah,' I muttered, embarrassed. 'I think – you know, right after A levels and everything. I think he's a bit shattered.'

'I just wish Ian would take a bit more – ' then she broke off and hugged me again, called out goodbye, and hurried down the path.

That's probably the last time I'll ever see her, I thought. And she's going to walk out of Art's life like that too. It seemed incredible that someone could just go like that, after more than four years; that it was the only choice they had.

Then I went back into the kitchen and faced Mum.

Thirty-two

'I really don't understand why you're so surprised by it all,' Mum said, a bit testily. 'I mean – I'm not completely stupid. I already knew Art's family's VERY LIBERAL views on what he got up to in his room. And since you were spending all the hours God sends round there, I took it you were fine about it too.'

'But aren't you – aren't you – '

'Aren't I what? Sad that you've discovered sex so young? Yes, a bit. But it's happened. And it was your choice this time. No good me trying to put a ban on you now, is there?'

'Well, no, but – '

'I'm a realist, Colette. And you seem to be being very mature about it. All I hope, every day, is that you won't get hurt.'

'But this holiday – '

'Sounds wonderful. What an opportunity. When I was seventeen I was still going to Scarborough with my parents.'

I stood and stared at her, almost speechless, and she looked back. 'What?' she said. 'You do WANT to go, don't you?'

We planned to have nearly four weeks in Greece. I couldn't believe it – I was so excited. I couldn't believe the way Mum had just handed me all that freedom, with her blessing. In my more honest moments I admitted to myself that I was even a little scared by it. It was like she'd said – Right, OK, you're an adult now. Sort of what Art's dad had said to him.

Once Art knew for sure that we were both going to Greece, he became almost manic. He used the empty house like a playground, spreading out into all of it. His friends got to hear about it and took to dropping in at all hours. Joe arrived with Rachel a couple of times, and we all lay about and played loud music together. One night, Art threw a riotous party that went on until the early hours; people were still strewn across the floors down-stairs when an estate agent came round the next day. Sometimes Art and I got sick of other people being around and we'd take off on our bikes. I loved that – I'd missed being outdoors with him.

The ferocious cleaning lady, who'd been coming to the house for years, still turned up once a week to 'muck out' as she called it, and she and Art would swear at each other over the state the place was in. She kept on at him about how they both had a responsibility to his dad to keep the place in order, but you could tell she was more on Art's side than Ian's. She'd mutter about people not giving a damn what their kids were up to, and nag Art to eat properly.

Art sorted out the travel arrangements for Greece. My airfare was to be my seventeenth birthday present from Mum and Dad. I was quite upset when it turned out the only flights we could get were on the day before my birthday – I'd imagined still being at home for that. When I broke the news to Mum, she gave me one of her huge, enveloping bear hugs and told me we'd celebrate it two days early.

'You were two days late getting yourself born anyway, dear,' she said, comfortably. 'So it's quite appropriate.' She said I could ask some friends along if I liked – or just Art – but I said no, and in the end only Mum, Dad, Sarah and I sat down to a big, squishy cream cake with fresh strawberries and lots of lemonade.

I felt quite weird as I went to bed that night, with my holiday packing all around me. I was thinking how fast events had moved in my seventeenth year. I used to stop and look at what went on in the world and think about it, but now I felt I was caught up in the fast stream, where you hardly got time to think at all.

Thirty-three

So Art and I got to Greece. And when I look back and remember how perfect the little white stone house was, it still makes me want to cry. As soon as we'd arrived and unlocked the door, it felt like ours. Ours. It was so sweet, so simple – one bedroom, one bathroom, a tiny kitchen and a little courtyard place, crammed with plants.

We dumped our rucksacks, and went straight down to the beach and swam and swam, alongside the rocks, under the great blue bowl of the sky. It was late afternoon but the sun was still hot enough to dry the salt on your skin. Art showed me how to use the freshwater shower by the beach café, and then we bought a couple of ice-cold beers and sat side by side drinking them, watching the sun drop towards the sea line.

We made our way back to the house and made love on the white cotton sheets, falling asleep just as the cicadas started up their strange whirring on the trees outside. When we woke up, it was night-time, and we got showered and dressed and wandered out through the tiny foreign streets, ravenously hungry, looking for somewhere to eat.

Everything we saw, everything around us, filled me with delight. I loved the warm night air, the stray cats, the white roofs ... Art got hold of my hand, towing me along, laughing at me because I wanted to stop and look at everything, and found the centre of the village. It was crowded with people, festive and happy. We found a spare table in among the lines outside a busy taverna, and sat opposite each other. I stared at Art as he studied the menu, and I thought: this has to be as good as it gets, because I honestly don't think I can contain much more.

The next morning was my birthday. I was woken by Art crashing around in the kitchen; then he appeared at the door, with a plate piled with croissants and two mugs of coffee. Before I could get over my delight he'd disappeared, and come back with a big bunch of crazy, exotic, purple flowers.

'Happy birthday,' he said. 'I got up seriously early to go and buy all this. You'd better be grateful.'

I laughed, and told him I was grateful. The only thing I could find big enough to hold the flowers was a huge chipped red enamel jug, which clashed brilliantly with the flowers. I set it in the centre of the courtyard table, where it dominated everything.

'I'm going to buy you a present too,' Art said. 'But you'd better choose it.'

The days passed by, every new day like some treasure chest to be plundered. Most of the time I felt as if I was drugged with pleasure and happiness, living only for the moment. We swam and sunbathed and grew brown together; we took rickety coastline buses and explored, we shopped in the tiny markets and cooked, and each night we slept side by side in the white bed, as though it was our right. True to his word Art bought me a birthday gift of a beautiful silver chain. One day on the beach I made him a bracelet out of some sea-washed string and a tiny stone with a hole in it, and he tied it on and didn't take it off again.

In the second week we began exploring further, sometimes so far afield that we'd sleep on the beach for the night. A few times we went off with a change of clothes in our backpacks, and walk for miles, roaming around, meeting weird people, getting into long conversations, not knowing where we'd eat or sleep, getting lost and finding our way again. It was exhilarating and scary, and I always felt glad to get back safe to the little stone house, but I was glad we'd gone too, glad we'd shared that kind of adventure.

We fought sometimes. I got frightened one day because he'd spent too long out by the rocks snorkelling and I thought he'd drowned; he got irritated with me going round to Fran's friends to phone home a couple of times a week. He'd get restless easily and accuse me of 'playing house' and want to take off somewhere. But there were so many good times it didn't matter. We didn't talk once about what would happen when we got back. The here and now was so good, it seemed irrelevant.

Then one day we realised we had less than a week left, and suddenly there was a shadow over the holiday. Art said, 'My exam results'll be waiting for me,' but he refused to phone up and find out what they were. That night we wandered down to a tatty little bar next to the harbour, and he got very drunk.

The next morning, I said, 'Art, it's going to be awful when you go to college.'

He shrugged 'If I go.'

'You will. I know you will. And then we'll hardly see each other.'

'Yeah, we can, Coll. If we want to, we will. What's the point in talking about it now. What's the point in planning anything.'

He was very far from making any kind of promise to me, any kind of commitment about the future. And I knew that was what I wanted now – I'd admitted it to myself, however scared it made me feel, to admit that. I would have promised him anything.

Two days before the end of the holiday, we made love on the terrace, with the hot breeze on our skins and the banana plant leaves swaying above us, and when I came, I heard myself crying 'I love you, I love you,' like some kind of chant. Art kissed me, again and again, but my words hung in the air, unanswered.

Thirty-four

Going home was so grim. Leaving all that beauty, all that freedom. It wouldn't have been so bad if Art had talked to me, if we could have discussed things a bit — almost if we could have mourned together. But I knew his response to feeling bad was to shut off, close down.

I was surprised by how glad I was to see Mum and Dad again, even Sarah. But in a weird way, it didn't feel like my home any more. I felt full of emptiness. It felt wrong to be here and not with Art. I was used to having him next to me, used to being able to stretch out my hand, and he'd be there. I missed him so much.

Two hours after I'd got home Art phoned to tell me that he'd got the grades he needed. I congratulated him, and suggested we get together that night to celebrate, but he said, 'Dad's here — I've got stuff to sort out with him about college.' When I asked if I could see him the next day, he said, 'Coll, we've just had *four weeks* together! What's the urgency? I'll see you when I've sorted this out, OK?'

I went up and sat in my room, and thought about going to sleep that night on my own, and I felt as if I were on the edge of a pit, looking into darkness. Then I went downstairs and phoned Rachel, and after a bit of small chat, I got Joe's phone number off her. Then I phoned Joe up, and told him I had to see him. I suppose it must have been the way I sounded that made him say yes right away. We agreed on a pub, two hours' time.

When I turned up he was already there in the corner, with his elbows on the table, hands propping up his face.

'Hi, Joe,' I said, 'thanks for saying you'd – 'Then I had to stop, because I could feel tears choking me.

'What's up?' asked Joe. 'Look – sit here. I'll get you a drink.'

While he was at the bar I pulled myself together with some severity. I hadn't come here for sympathy, I'd come for inside information. As soon as he'd sat down and I'd thanked him for the drink and he'd told me how brown I was, I took a deep breath and said, 'Do you think it's possible – that two people can be together, and have a great time, I mean, have something really special together – and it means a lot more to one than it does the other? Don't answer that. Of course it's possible. What I mean is – if someone tells you you're special to them, and you *know* you are – but it still doesn't mean that much to them? It's not that big a deal to them?'

There was a pause, then Joe said, 'Why d'you think it doesn't mean that much?'

'Because – because he never says anything, because he

never – oh, shit. It's like we're doing the same things, and it means so much to me, and – I just don't *know* what it means to him. We've just had this most amazing holiday, and I feel – I can't tell you how I feel. It's so awful, being back. It's awful. The only thing that would make it a bit more bearable would be to get to see *him*. But he said he's busy, and we'd been together for four weeks, so why did we need to see each other so soon?'

Joe shrugged. 'Well, he's got a lot on with going to college, I mean I'm – '

'I feel like we were on different *holidays*. I was on this fantastic, magic thing, that meant so much, and he was – oh, *shit*. I used to really *despise* girls who had to have little tokens of love all the time. You know – phone calls every day, and presents, and celebrating your three-month anniversary – I used to think it was so fake – like they created the *relationship* through all that. And people who made promises – "we'll be together for ever and ever" – I used to think they were mad. But now I – now I – '

'Now you could do with some of it?'

'Yes. No. Oh, God, I don't know. It's just – there's nothing to hold *on* to! Sometimes I *know* how much I mean to him, I just know it. But other times, it's like he's shut me out – and – and I've got no right to be upset about it. It's like he won't let things *progress* – he won't let anything *grow*. He's gone all distant on me again, talking about heading off to college as though, well, you just get on with it, but I know it's going to tear me *apart* – '

'Maybe he knows it'll tear him apart too.'

'Well if he does he does a bloody good job of hiding it. He's all cold and – *efficient*. And I miss him so much I – oh, I don't know. I don't know if he's just not *saying*

190

stuff to me, or …or not *feeling* it, not feeling anything.'

'Maybe he's putting up barriers, protecting himself.'

'But *why*? Why can't he *talk* about things?'

'Well – maybe he's feeling stuff he can't even admit to himself, let alone you.'

'*Why not*? Why can't he just let himself *feel*, why can't he –'

'Coll, most blokes aren't good at that sort of thing. And Art – well, he's worse. He's damaged. You know that.'

When he said that word 'damaged', I felt this weird chill go through me, as if something I'd half understood was going to be clear at last. 'Damaged?' I whispered. 'What d'you mean?'

Joe shrugged. 'Think about it. His mum died when he was a kid, and his dad just took off – left him. What d'you think that did to him?'

'Well I know, I know, but –'

'When people fight just to survive, it does things to them. I mean – you have to sit on all sorts of stuff just to get through the day. He – sees people differently. He's a loner – he's not open like most people are.'

I was silent, staring at the table. Joe was staring at it too. Then he said, 'Look, when he started at our school, we all thought he was so cool. He'd been kicked out of boarding school, and he drank, and he did drugs, and he *slept with women*! But there was a part of him you didn't trust. Oh, everyone wanted to hang around with him, but not many people got close.' He took a long swig of beer. 'When I first met you – at that really snobby party? I felt sorry for you. You might have copped off with the best-looking guy in the room, but I knew what a shit he could be.'

'But you were *close*,' I croaked. 'You were good friends.

And I thought you were starting to be again – '

He shrugged. 'I wouldn't ever get that tied up with him again. I could see the way he treated people sometimes, and I didn't like it, but I never thought he'd do it to me. Then when he did – '

I'd started crying again. Joe put his arm round me awkwardly. 'Hey. It's not that bad. Look – I'm not saying he's just going to dump you or anything. You've outlasted any other girl he's been out with by *months* – '

'Oh, big deal,' I wailed. 'What's the point if it's all just going to end – and I'm going to get hurt – and – '

'Look, Coll – you know what I think? You scare him shitless. That's why he's backing off now, that's why he won't commit to anything. He's scared of getting to depend on you.'

'*Why* is he? I depend on him. Why can't he just *trust* me and – '

'Most people are scared to trust. Especially people who've lost people, like Art did. And now Fran's going – '

'He didn't like her much though,' I sniffed. 'He called her Frankenstein.'

'Yeah, but she was there. She made a home for him. He used it and abused it, but it was there – and now even that's going – '

'Well he's got *me*! Or he could have. I could help him, I could ... '

'If he lets you. He's scared of letting you. He's not exactly been shown the joys of monogamy, has he, with his past history. He thinks the only person he can rely on is himself. He's scared of letting you in too close.' There was another pause, and then Joe said, 'Have you told him?'

'What?'

'What you feel for him?'

'Yes. Sort of. He knows. He must know.'

'Like you know what he feels?'

'No, more than that. I've tried to tell him but he shuts me up when I try to say anything. He doesn't want to hear it. I can see it in his face.'

Joe sighed. 'Oh, Coll. You've got it bad, haven't you?'

'Yes. Like an illness.'

'Lovesickness.'

'Maybe.'

'I *know* he's gone on you too.'

'Why? What's he said?

'Oh come on, he hasn't *said* anything. It's just – the way he is with you, the fact you're still together. I mean – just *that's* extraordinary, for him.'

When Joe said that, I felt this determination flood into me. 'I can't go on like this, not being straight about what I feel,' I said. 'I can't bear the thought of him going away, and it being all "see you when I see you, no point in making plans".'

'Well, you'll just have to face him with it, won't you? Tell him. And if you tell him what you feel for him, it could go either way. Either he'll start to trust you and open up himself – or – '

'Or I'll scare him off for good,' I said.

Thirty-five

We chewed it all over a bit more, and I felt a whole lot better for just being able to speak to someone who knew Art, and for reaching some kind of a decision inside myself. Joe said he'd give me a lift home, and as we drove along, I said, 'You're pretty clued up for a bloke, aren't you?'

He laughed. 'When Art got off with Janey, I was so screwed up about it my mum made me go and talk to one of her friends – someone who was training to be a therapist. She practised on me.'

'God, how embarrassing.'

'No, it was OK once it got going. I didn't know her, it was like – isolated – and we really talked. She decided pretty quickly that Art was the one with problems, not me. We talked about him a lot. I mean – she thought he needed help, her kind of help.'

'And did you tell him that?

'No. At the time, I wouldn't've helped him if he'd been on fire, and I'd had an extinguisher. I hated him.'

I laughed. 'The therapy didn't work there, then.'

'Well, I s'pose it made me understand him a bit better. But I still felt so angry with him I could've killed him. This woman told me to play a lot of hard sport, pretend the ball was Art, that kind of stuff. Look Coll – '

'What?'

'You've got to tell him what you feel. You've got to sort it out. He won't.'

When I woke up the next day, I felt brave, determined. I knew I'd reached the crossroads. I was going to tell him everything I felt about him, make or break. The minute it got to ten o'clock, I phoned Art.

He answered, blearily. And as soon as I'd said hello, there was his voice, in my ear, swearing, hissing, ugly. An obscene spurt of rage that had no sense, no meaning. Then the phone went dead.

My fingers pressed the redial button automatically. Everything in me was on hold, except for my heart, which was pounding.

It rang twice, then it was cut off. I redialled, and got the engaged signal.

I wasn't angry – I was scared. I wondered what could have happened, to make him act like that. I thought of drugs, drink, evil cocktails, overdoses. I thought his dad might have come back, and had a fight with him, sent him over the edge. I thought of all the causes except for the real one.

I shot round to his house and hammered on the door.

He opened it, and again, there was this stream of swearing, so extreme, so bizarre that it didn't even occur to me to be offended. I got my shoulder in the door as he started to slam it on me, and barged my way into the hall.

'Don't you shut me out,' I shouted. 'Don't you *dare* shut me out. What the hell's going on?'

'Maybe you should tell ME that. Bitch.'

'Jesus, Art, what is going *on*?'

'Did you have a nice time with him? Good lay, is he?'

'What the *hell* are you talking about?'

'How long you been seeing him?'

'What the *hell* − ' And then it all became clear to me, that Art must have somehow seen me with Joe last night, and for a second I felt almost guilty. 'Art, look, I can explain,' I said as calmly as I could manage. 'I phoned Joe up because I − '

'I saw you in his car. You were having a real laugh.'

'Oh, look. We went out for a drink together. I've never done it before. I asked him because − I needed to talk to him. About *you*.'

'Sure you did.'

'I *did*! You were being so ... weird, and I − '

'*Sure* you did.'

'Art, will you *stop* this? We were talking about *you*. He's the only person I know who knows *you*.'

Art turned contemptuously and headed up the stairs to his room. I followed, shouting, 'You're behaving like a moron, Art! There's no law that says I can't see one of your friends, is there?'

I went along the landing, pushed into his room. 'Well, is there?'

'Get out of my room.'

'Jesus will you *grow up*. I can't believe what's going through your stupid mind. I was upset – I was upset because you'd got all closed off, since we'd got back, and I wanted to talk to someone who *knows* you, understands what you –'

'Sure, Coll, sure,' he sneered. 'It looked like you were talking about that, from where I was. It really did.'

'God, you're so *stupid*,' I shouted. I felt like hitting him. He was so wrong it was insane. I went and stood right in front of him and I didn't know what to do, what to say. I felt faint, like you do when you're standing on top of a huge waterfall, staring down at the crashing water beneath.

Then it was like I jumped.

'D'you want to know what we were talking about?' I said. 'D'you want to? I was telling him I'm in *love* with you, OK? I was saying how much I *feel* for you – how much that *scares* me. How we need to start *talking* about it, because it's the most important thing that's ever happened to me.'

I stopped, drew breath. I felt terrified, saying all this at last. I felt terrific.

'I'd *never* cheat on you, never,' I went on. 'I'd never want to. Don't you *know* that? We have the most amazing holiday together, and – and then you just come home and switch off – and I can't *bear* the thought of you going away, I can't bear it. All I can think about is *you*, and wanting to be with *you* – it's like I'm *nothing* if I'm on my own.'

Art was staring at me. There was a long beat of silence. It was too long. He didn't move. 'You scare the shit out of me when you talk like that,' he muttered, finally.

'You're scared?' I breathed, through my cracked throat. '*You're* scared? I'm scared. I'm scared I feel a lot more than you do ... I'm scared of never seeing you again. I'm scared you're the one – I'm scared I'll *never* get over you, *never*, I'll never stop loving you, and no one I meet will come up to you – '

Art was looking away. He wouldn't look at me. He wouldn't move. I couldn't move. I felt so sick I thought I was going to puke on the floor. I wanted to cry and whimper. I wanted to say – please love me, Art, please love me.

And then I saw them. Earrings, on the table by his bed. They were dull silver, with hooks on, very elegant. Not mine. I don't wear earrings.

It was like everything had slowed down, like those moments before the truck hits the dog, the child falls from the window. There's nothing you can do – the tragedy is already in place.

'Whose are those?' I croaked, pointing.

Then without waiting to hear, I walked out of the room, and went into the bathroom. I crouched over the pan and retched and retched. Then I collapsed on the floor.

Art came in and sat beside me. He put his hands on my shoulders and tried to lift me. Then he stood up and got me a drink of water, and came and sat beside me again.

'Coll,' he said, 'Coll, nothing happened. When I saw you with Joe I just – I flipped. I couldn't stand what I was feeling. I went and got drunk, I was out of it. Then I went – I went round to this girl's house, someone I used to – and ... she came out with me, and we ended up back here.'

He stopped and pushed the hair away from my face. I let him. I felt so leaden I could hardly move.

'Then I just passed out. I heard her get up in the night and leave and I made out I was asleep so I wouldn't have to talk to her.'

'It doesn't matter,' I whispered. 'What difference does it make?'

He reached out and put his arms round me. I tried to push him away, then I let him pull me in against him. It was like wanting water when you're parched, even if you know the water's poisoned, polluted.

'We've got to stop this,' I said, 'We've got to end this now. I can't take any more of this.'

There was a long silence. I felt completely numb, as though I were looking down at us from a distance. I knew that sometime soon that numbness would go, and the pain would start, and I'd need all my strength to deal with it. And I knew I had to talk now while I could see us clearly, I had to get it all straight now before all the need and pain and wanting came in again and confused everything.

'You seeing me with Joe – you picking up that girl – it doesn't matter,' I said. 'What matters is you don't want to be involved with me, not like ... not like I want. You don't feel like I feel. You'll go to college and you'll have loads of girls after you – and this'll happen again – and – and I'm not going through this any more. If I stay with you I'll get so hurt I – '

He didn't speak. I pulled away from him and wiped my eyes.

You know what I feel now, anyway,' I went on. 'I meant it. I meant everything I said. I'd – I'd *love* someone to feel about me the way I feel about you.' I paused, and looked at him. 'Maybe you do underneath. Maybe that's why you freaked when you saw us in the car together. You just can't admit it.' I felt a sort of bleak triumph, a dead triumph, as I realised that. 'You won't let me in, will you? You can't.'

'I can't handle it, Coll,' he said, in a low voice. 'I'm sorry. I'm just not – I'm not ready for all this.'

My throat was so tight I felt someone was strangling me. We sat there on the bathroom floor together, and it was like death, it was like we couldn't move.

'I'm no good for you,' he said at last. 'I can't be what you want. You're so open, You're so emotional – I don't know how you do that. I don't know how you risk that. I love being with you, you know that. I loved that holiday. But it's over, and we've got to do our own things now – ' He trailed off and let out a long, shaky sigh. 'I was so screwed up last night it scared me. I'm not ready for it, Coll. I'm sorry. *You* scare me. I'm just not – ready.'

I sat there for a while longer, and in my head I was rehearsing standing up, walking out of the door, down the stairs. I wasn't sure I could do it.

Then at last I did stand up, and make my way towards the door.

'Coll, I'm sorry,' he said again. I didn't answer. Somehow, I got to the top of the stairs, and went down them, and out of the front door. Then I closed it behind me.

Thirty-six

Something as bad as that — it's like a death, an assassination. I thought I was going to go mad in the days that followed. I was so scared of the pit of misery that had opened up under me. For the first few days I just cried and cried. I kept hearing the sound of the door as I closed it after me, and the silence when he didn't come after me. Then I got numb, like someone sick who has a great wound inside, and it takes all their energy just to live with that wound. It was the worst of times, the end of that summer, the start of the new term.

I hung on to knowing I'd done the right thing, I'd acted with courage. It wasn't much to hang on to, but it was something. When I felt at my weakest, at my most tempted to get in touch with him again, I'd make myself think what it would be like to be still sort-of together — because I think we could still have been sort-of together, if I'd backed off, made no demands of him. It would have been all hope and need on my side, and nothing I could trust on his. I thought of living from one visit to the next, one phone call to the next, one letter to the next; how I'd get hurt again, over some girl, and maybe this time I wouldn't be strong enough to heal.

I threw myself into my work. It had been my sense of survival that had made me back away from Art – well, now I was going to do more than just survive. I knew what A level grades I needed for the university course I wanted to do, and I went at them, head on. Sometimes I felt almost proud of myself for coping so well, and that helped a bit too.

When I felt really bad, I'd go and see Val, and just to be with her made me feel better. One Saturday I found her in her room, gloomily trying to work. She was wading through a book, thick as a doorstep, with *Celtic Myths* on its spine.

'Isn't it daft the way the old stories can't deal with sex?' she grumbled. 'Death, yes, truckloads of it. But not sex.'

'I've got a theory about that,' I said eagerly.

'You would have.'

'Instead of sex, they had love potions.'

'What are you on about?'

'In the old fairy stories. And – you know – *Midsummer's Night's Dream* and stuff. You were tricked into drinking this stuff, and it made you fall in love with someone. It was really sex.'

'Coll – you're insane. There's no bonking in these old stories. I'd have noticed.'

'That's the *point* – it's in code. They couldn't talk about sex directly so they made it into a thingy, a – you know

– a metaphor. When they talked about the power of love potions they were really talking about the power of sex. Love potions led you to your doom, made you obsessed with people, blind to their faults – just like sex. You fall for them even if they're awful, even if they have ass's ears, even if they're – ' I broke off.

'If they're what?' said Val, gently.

I could feel myself sighing. 'Wrong for you,' I said.

I got used to it. I got used to feeling unhappy most of the time, shutting everything out. I went out with my friends occasionally. Val and Greg were still together, just. Things hadn't worked out for Rachel and Joe, and they'd split up, too, a month after he'd gone to university. There was a kind of wintry gloom over everyone, as we went from October into November.

'Do you regret it?' Val said one day. 'Getting involved at all I mean? If you could just make it so you'd never met him, would you?'

'No,' I said, surprised by how quickly I'd replied.

And I didn't wish it hadn't happened, that was the weird thing. I was glad for how much I'd felt for him, how special it had been. And I didn't feel used, tricked, betrayed, any of those things. It had finished because Art hadn't been able to cope with it, that was all.

As the months passed the first absolute anguish faded, but I missed him so badly still. It was like there was an ache of missing him, there all the time, and sometimes things would make me forget it for an hour or two, but it would still be there, it would always make itself felt. I wouldn't let myself think back about our time together. It was too dangerous. I hid the few photos I had right at the back of my wardrobe.

I wore the silver chain he'd bought me, though. I never took it off.

As Christmas got close and I knew he'd be breaking up for the holidays I found myself burning up with curiosity, wanting to know what had happened to him. Maybe he'd met someone new, and she was just as special to him now as I'd been. The thing that really hurt was imagining he'd got over me quickly. I found myself yearning to talk to him, continue that heart-killing conversation we'd had on the floor of his bathroom, find out if I'd meant as much to him as he'd done to me.

Maybe I'll get in touch with him over the holidays, I thought, and we can meet and talk calmly. I've got nothing to lose now, after all. But just the thought terrified me.

Thirty-seven

I wasn't looking forward to the Christmas holidays at all. I was scared of not having the punishing, regular routine of school to keep me on track, scared of feeling overwhelmed by all the conspicuous happiness round about me. I'd read a statistic somewhere that there were more suicides at Christmas than at any other time in the year.

Val and Caro got me by the throat, practically, on the last day of term and told me we were going to have fun over the holidays. They'd planned a party and a club tour already. I knew I had no option, so I tried to look keen.

The day after we broke up, Mum dragged me off into town shopping, saying she wanted to buy me some clothes to cheer me up. It was very sweet of her to think of it, and brain-numbingly awful to do. I didn't want clothes; and I didn't want to be in among a load of festive shoppers – I would have been far happier curled up reading at home. But Mum, as always, refused to take no for an answer.

Once we were out, we were both so polite to each other it was unnatural. She was horribly patient with me. I tried on things I hated just to please her, and forced myself to seem enthusiastic over all the Christmas displays when really they depressed the hell out of me.

We were just leaving our seventh clothes shop discussing whether we should have lunch now or in half an hour or so – both wanting to do what the other wanted to do – when I stopped short. I'd seen Joe, coming out of a record shop. He was on his own.

My heart turned over, literally, at the sight of him. He was my link, the only person I knew who knew Art. I told Mum to give me five minutes, and headed over to him, stopping right in front of him. I felt myself wanting to get hold of him by the lapels and shout in his face, 'Has Art met someone else? Has he?'

'Coll!' he said, pleased. 'How *are* you?'

'OK. How's university?'

'All right. Good to get home though. There's just so much to get used to at first. I'm in these really grim digs and – '

I watched his mouth move as he described his digs, his new friends. I heard nothing. I wondered how quickly I could interrupt and ask about Art.

'Joe,' I said at last, 'have you heard anything from Art?'

He looked at me strangely. 'Haven't you heard?'

I could feel my pulse racing. 'Heard – what?'

'He had some kind of a – I dunno. Crack up. Five weeks into college. He just – went off.'

'Went off?'

'He drew out all his grant, and just went. As far as his dad knows, he's in New Zealand somewhere.'

'New *Zealand*?! *What happened*?'

Joe was looking at me, hard. 'He went on a complete wrecker after you broke up. I saw him a couple of times. He was in a state. He made me swear not to – '

'Not to what?'

'Not to get in touch with you. Otherwise I would've. I mean, he really wanted to see you Coll, I know he did. Then he went to college, and I lost touch. I tried to get him by phone a couple of times, but he was always out. Then I heard that he'd just – gone. I phoned his dad's company in the end. He thinks he's in New Zealand, but he hasn't heard anything from him for weeks.'

I thought of Art on a beach somewhere, watching the sun go down. 'How will he live?' I said.

'Oh, he took a lot of cash with him. And he'll work – jobs in bars and stuff. He used to go on about having a year off, before college, but his dad was dead against it. Ian just wanted to get him on the ladder going up. I think it's great, he's gone. Just travelling the world, working your way. I wish I'd gone with him.'

'Did he ask you to?'

'Well – no. I mean – it didn't come up. I think he wanted to be on his own.'

I gazed ahead of me, down the rows of bright shops with all their tinsel and coloured lights, and realised there was no way I could get in touch with Art now, and I felt suddenly glad, suddenly free of something. 'That's great,' I said. 'I hope he finds what he's looking for.'

'Well – I'd better be going,' Joe announced abruptly,

and I realised Mum had come over and was standing in earshot. He told me to give him a ring sometime, and said he'd phone me if he heard anything more. Then we said goodbye.

Mum and I walked off slowly, then she suddenly turned to me and hissed, 'Don't you DARE start romanticising this!'

'What are you talking about?' I answered.

'You're smiling! What are you smiling about? I know you! You'll be imagining all kinds of nonsense about WHY Art went off, thinking it's to do with what happened with you ... ' She wound down, and I knew it was because she was thinking that too.

'Oh, Mum,' I said. 'I'm just glad he's done it, that's all.'

'Me too,' she said surprisingly. 'He needed to get away. From that appalling father of his for one thing, and – '

'And me?' I interrupted.

'Oh, darling, no. Just – I always thought you were a bit mature for him. He needed to sort himself out.'

There was a silence as we walked along, then Mum said, 'If I catch you hanging round the front door, waiting for letters with New Zealand postmarks – '

I burst out laughing. 'That hadn't even occurred to me,' I said. 'I've got my own life to lead. I've got exams to get before I take off round the world.'

'Before you WHAT? Don't you start getting ideas about – '

'Oh, Mum, shut up, will you? Come on. Let's go back to those tops we were looking at. Maybe I'll let you buy me one after all.'

Mum sniffed. 'Big of you. Anyway, I want lunch now.'

'Well, too bad. Let's get that top first. I've got some serious partying to do over the next couple of weeks.'

Then I linked my arm through hers and towed her back the way we'd come.

grab a livewire!

real life, real issues, real books, real bite

Rebellion, rows, love and sex . . . pushy boyfriends, fussy parents, infuriating brothers and pests of sisters . . . body image, trust, fear and hope . . . homelessness, bereavement, friends and foes . . raves and parties, teachers and bullies . . . identity, culture clash, tension and fun . . . abuse, alcoholism, cults and survival . . . fat thighs, hairy legs, hassle and angst . . . music, black issues, media and politics . . . animal rights, environment, veggies and travel . . . taking risks, standing up, shouting loud and breaking out . . .

. . . grab a Livewire!

For a free copy of our latest catalogue,
send a stamped addressed envelope to:

The Sales Department
Livewire Books
The Women's Press Ltd
34 Great Sutton Street
London EC1V 0DX
Tel: 0171 251 3007
Fax: 0171 608 1938

Also of interest:

Kate Cann
Diving In

'As the hot water pounded down on me I was suddenly aware that I was not alone. Someone was standing very close to me, under the same shower. I opened my eyes, blinking away water. It was him . . .'

Colette daydreams all the time about meeting the gorgeous bloke she sees at her local swimming pool. Then one afternoon, he asks her out. Close-up, he's more good-looking – but he's also very pushy.

As Coll struggles to get what she wants from their relationship, she begins to wonder just how far she should go. Can she cope with a boyfriend who's much more experienced than her? How much should she suppress what she's increasingly feeling? Will she turn out like her man-hating mum – or like Art's sad last girlfriend who suddenly got dumped? Just how fast should Coll be diving into love?

Young Adult Fiction £3.99
ISBN 0 7043 4937 X

Lois Keith

A Different Life

Libby Starling can't wait for the school trip to come. But what is she going to wear? Will Cleo ignore her again? And what about quiet, confident Jesse – will he notice her at last?

A week later, it is impossible for Libby to believe that this was all she had to worry about. Because after the school trip, everything has changed.

After a swim in the sea, Libby becomes mysteriously ill. Everyone seems to know what's best for her – doctors, physiotherapists, parents, the headteacher. Libby realises that she must choose what is important to her now. She learns how to be strong, and, with the help of those who love her, she starts to live a new, different life . . .

'As with the best novels, I did not want this story to end.' *Sunday Times*

'Can be enjoyed by young disabled people and non-disabled people . . . grab a copy, spend some time with lively Elizabeth Starling, and see for yourself.' *DIAL*

'A wonderful book.' *Disability Times*

Young Adult Fiction £5.99
ISBN 0 7043 4946 9

Nadya Kassam, editor

Telling It Like It Is
Young Asian Women Talk

'You're always saying that I'll be lucky to get married and have children, the way I am. Is that what you think? That I will spend my life just as somebody's wife, with no identity of my own, content to look after the house and stay in the kitchen all day? Do you really think that all Asian wives need to keep them happy is a new microwave? The answer is NO! I don't know which century you are living in, but I'm telling you one thing for sure – being an Asian woman is not a punishment or a restriction. The world is my oyster and my life will be what I make it!'

Boyfriends versus cultural and spiritual values; looking good and fitting in at school or dressing as Mum, Dad and religion dictate; parties and clubs or homework and studies; arranged marriages or 'love matches'. In this passionate and lively collection, young Asian women struggle against restrictions, stick up for their culture, express frustrations and joys, describe the impact of racism on their lives, balance two cultures, and search for the most fulfilling ways of living. Telling It Like It Is is a fascinating, hilarious, moving, powerful and exhilarating read.

Young Adult Non-Fiction £4.99
ISBN 0 7043 4941 8

Lesléa Newman

Fat Chance

'Dear Diary,

Today Ms Roth, our new English teacher, gave us all notebooks and said we were all to keep a diary. She said writing in a diary is something you do for your own personal growth. I could do with a little less personal growth. You're supposed to weigh 100 pounds if you're five feet tall, and add five pounds for every inch. So, I should weigh 120 pounds, but I'd like to get down to 115 . . .'

So begins the often humorous, often painful private diary of Judi. Worried that she'll never lose weight and wondering if Richard Weiss will ever ask her out, Judi has a lot on her mind. Then her new diet starts to work, and Judi decides to eat less and less . . .

'Genuinely funny. A fabulous book which I recommend without reservation.' *Los Angeles Times*

Young Adult Fiction £3.50
ISBN 0 7043 4934 5

What the judges and media have said about Livewire:

Livewire Books have won:

The Other Award
The Red Fist and Silver Slate Pencil Award
The Council on Interracial Books Award
The National Conference of Christians and Jews Mass Media Award
The Lewis Carroll Shelf Award

and much, much more.

The press has said:

'outstanding' *Vogue*
'stupendous' *Guardian*
'outrageously funny' *7 Days*
'hugely enjoyable' *British Book News*
'compulsively witty' *Times Literary Supplement*
'riotous and down-to-earth' *Africa World Review*
'genuinely funny' *Los Angeles Times*
'explosive . . . exceptional' *Times Literary Supplement*
'brilliant' *Observer*
'riotous' *Times Educational Supplement*

grab a livewire!
save £££s!!! with this voucher

Buy any of the following books and get
£1 off each book you buy! Post-free!

Diving In by Kate Cann
A Different Life by Lois Keith
Telling It Like It Is
Young Asian Women Talk edited by Nadya Kassam
Fat Chance by Lesléa Newman

See previous pages for descriptions

Name _____

Address _____

_____

_____

Postcode _____

I would like:

_____ copies of **Diving In** at £3.99 less £1 = £2.99

_____ copies of **A Different Life** at £5.99 less £1 = £4.99

_____ copies of **Telling It Like It Is** at £4.99 less £1 = £3.99

_____ copies of **Fat Chance** at £3.50 less £1 = £2.50

_____ Livewire catalogue

Total enclosed £ _____

Do not send cash through the post. Send postal orders (from the Post Office)
in pounds sterling or cheques made out to The Women's Press.

Send this form and your cheque or postal order to The Women's Press,
34 Great Sutton Street, London EC1V 0DX. Allow up to 28 days for delivery.
Do remember to fill in your name and address!

This offer applies only in the UK to the books listed above, subject to availability.
This voucher cannot be exchanged for cash. Cash value 0.0001p